Praise for
I CRAWL THROUGH IT

○○○○● ●○○○○ ○○●○○ ○●○○○ ○○○○●

"*I Crawl Through It* proves that A.S. King is one of the
most innovative and talented novelists of our time.
This is King's masterpiece—a brilliant, paranoid, poetic,
funny, and at times overwhelmingly sad literary cocktail
of absinthe and Adderall. What a trip!"
—Andrew Smith, acclaimed author of *Winger* and *Grasshopper Jungle*

"King's devotion to **a passionately experimental style,** in a genre
often beholden to formula, is inspiring. **Kurt Vonnegut might have
written a book like this.**"
—*The New York Times Book Review*

"A.S. King has penned an absorbing Rorschach test of
a book that, as you turn its pages, manages to read you....
I Crawl Through It presents the shattered perspective,
the moment when young minds unspool like line from
a broken fishing reel.... **I assigned this book an A.**"
—*Entertainment Weekly*

★ "Characters unfold like riddles before the reader....
Beautiful prose, poetry, and surreal imagery combine
for **an utterly original story** that urges readers to question, love,
and believe—or risk explosion."
—*Booklist*, starred review

★ **"Ambitious and affecting** work.... 'Somewhere in every mind,' the last pages of the book assert, 'is an opening to crawl through.' King's latest novel demands that readers search for this opening."
—*The Horn Book*, starred review

★ "Bizarre, compelling, and **not like anything else.**"
—*Publishers Weekly*, starred review

★ "[A.S. King] achieves a fine, delicate balance through her gutting prose and ensemble cast of hurt-filled characters. At once a statement on the culture of modern schools as well as mental health issues, this novel is **an ambitious, haunting work of art.**"
—*SLJ*, starred review

★ "Under all of the strangeness, magic, and metaphor, this is a story about fear, shame, guilt, lies, truth, trauma, escape, and rescue. It is a story about constantly seeking answers, even when you cannot articulate the questions.... And it is about the hardest test of all: surviving adolescence. **Masterfully written and brilliantly bizarre**, this is King at her most innovative yet."
—*VOYA*, starred review

"A meditation on grief, guilt, and survival.... Readers [will be] rewarded with the self-actualization of finely wrought characters.... **Absolutely worthwhile**."
—*Kirkus Reviews*

I CRAWL THROUGH IT

A NOVEL BY
A.S. KING

LITTLE, BROWN AND COMPANY
NEW YORK ◆ BOSTON

Text copyright © 2015 by A.S. King
Illustrations copyright © 2015 by Wendy Xu
Discussion Guide copyright © 2015 by Little, Brown and Company

Little, Brown and Company

Hachette Book Group
1290 Avenue of the Americas, New York, NY 10104
Visit us at lb-teens.com

Little, Brown and Company is a division of Hachette Book Group, Inc.
The Little, Brown name and logo are trademarks of Hachette Book Group, Inc.

The publisher is not responsible for websites (or their content) that are not owned by the publisher.

First Paperback Edition: August 2016
First published in hardcover in September 2015 by Little, Brown and Company

The Library of Congress has cataloged the hardcover edition as follows:

King, A. S. (Amy Sarig), 1970–
    I crawl through it / by A.S. King. — First edition.
        pages cm
    Summary: "A surrealist novel about four teenagers who find unconventional ways to escape standardized tests and their perilous world, and discover that the only escape from reality is to face it"— Provided by publisher.
    ISBN 978-0-316-33409-9 (hardcover) — ISBN 978-0-316-33407-5 (ebook) — ISBN 978-0-316-33410-5 (library edition ebook) [1. Reality—Fiction.] I. Title.
    PZ7.K5693Iak 2015   [Fic]—dc23   2014036896

Paperback ISBN 978-0-316-33408-2

10 9 8 7 6 5 4 3 2

LSC-C

Printed in the United States of America

For Andrea Spooner

What is a weed? A plant whose virtues have yet to be discovered.
—Ralph Waldo Emerson

Prologue—The place
where we explain the
helicopter and how not
to eat the green sauce at
Las Hermanas and we
don't mention anything
about love

Gustav is building a helicopter. Nobody knows because Gustav has been building it in small sections. He understands things like the physics of flight. He understands vectors.

I could never understand a science that doesn't relate to humans or biology; but Gustav tells me his helicopter will be better than a stupid human.

He says, "Can *you* fly?"

○○○●○

Gustav believes his helicopter is invisible, and because he believes it, it is so.

There are two seats in Gustav's invisible helicopter so he can take a passenger. There is space behind the seats so he can take a backpack. Snacks. A camera. A helicopter map. Maybe a parachute. Maybe no parachute. It probably depends on his destination.

"This isn't some dumb mini-helicopter kit," he said when he explained it at first. "It cost me fifty grand."

"Where did you get that kind of money?" I asked.

"None of your business," he said.

○○○○●

Gustav is building a red helicopter. It's not invisible. If I want, I can see it on Tuesdays. Other people can see it on other days, but I can only see it on Tuesdays, which is when the #10 combo is the dinner special at Las Hermanas. My favorite. *Dos enchiladas.* Always get the red sauce. The green will burn your eyes out.

Gustav lives three blocks from Las Hermanas, so I stop by and see the helicopter on my way home. He is making good progress.

Mama says Gustav is mad crazy. I think he's a genius. I think Mama is jealous. I think she would build a helicopter and take off as soon as she could if she could, but she can't so she doesn't and she says lies about Gustav like "That boy isn't right in the head" or "He's going to end up in the looney tunes if he's not careful."

Stanzi Has a Family History

Mama and Pop went on a trip this week. Usually they save the trips for weekends or summer vacation with me, but they said they wanted to go alone and asked if I could heat up my own TV dinners and stay safe overnight by myself. I'm a senior in high school. Raised by them. I heat up my own TV dinners and stay safe overnight every day by myself. I didn't say it that way to them, though. I just said yes.

So on Tuesday morning, they set their GPS for Newtown, Connecticut. That's where the 2012 Sandy Hook massacre was. I bet you could scan Mama's camera and I bet you'd find pictures of all the landmarks that were on TV. The firehouse. The neighbor's house. The school's parking lot. I bet you'd find a hundred damp, balled-up tissues on the floor of Pop's Buick, too.

It's like they're mourning the loss of me and I'm still alive.

It's like they're mourning the loss of something bigger than all of us and they take me with them to show me the hole. I've already been to Columbine, Virginia Tech, the site of that Amish school, and Red Lake, Minnesota. We even flew to Dunblane, Scotland, when I was ten.

I own the most morbid snow globe collection in the world.

For what it's worth, I can't lay one more cheap bouquet of flowers by a memorial. I can't light one more candle. I can't count out twenty fluffy teddy bears that will only wilt under the Connecticut winter snows.

For what it's worth, I sobbed for three days after that guy shot up those kids in Newtown. I stopped using tissues because my nose got so raw. I didn't shower. I didn't talk. I didn't breathe, hardly. Call me emotional or a drama queen and I don't care. I'll tell you again: I fucking sobbed.

Then I dissected a frog.

It didn't make me feel any better, but it made me stop crying.

Stanzi—Thursday—
Another Frog Dissection

1. Place frog in tray, ventral side up.
2. With forceps, lift the skin of the lower abdomen. Cut with scissors.
3. Slide scissors into the opening and cut to below the lower jaw.
4. Cut the sides just posterior to the forelimbs and anterior to the hind limbs.

This is my seventh frog dissection this year. Mr. Bio lets me help with the freshmen if they're dissecting. I am the best frog surgeon he knows. That's our joke. I bet he'd make me a name tag that says BEST FROG SURGEON if he could, but he's not very artistic. I'm his assistant, and I help hand out the forceps and scalpels while the students get into their lab coats and put on their goggles. I can't actually hand out the frogs, though, because I'm always surprised by how dead they are.

Lifeless.

Gray-green.

Bred so we could cut them open and find their livers and draw them for points in a notebook.

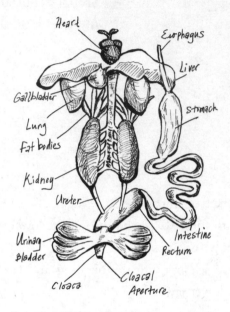

Mr. Bio told me in ninth grade, "You're going to make an excellent doctor one day."

"That's the plan," I said.

"It's a good plan."

"I want to help people," I said.

"Good."

"I know I can't help everybody, but even if I can help just one person, you know?"

"Yep," he said.

"I'm thinking about going into the army," I said.

Mr. Bio made a horrible face. "Why?"

"Did you ever watch *M*A*S*H*?" I answered. *M*A*S*H* is a late-twentieth-century TV show about a mobile army surgical hospital unit during the Korean War. It reruns on cable a lot. The main character is Benjamin Franklin "Hawkeye" Pierce. He's a surgeon from Maine.

"Of course," Mr. Bio said. "I grew up with *M*A*S*H*."

"That's why," I said. I didn't tell him Hawkeye Pierce is my mother. No one would understand that. Hawkeye Pierce was a man. A fictional man. Most people would think he couldn't be anyone's mother. Except he's mine. He puts me to bed every night. He makes my dinner. He teaches me about the world and he's always honest.

Mr. Bio put his hand on my shoulder and said, "You should stay away from that recruiter."

"It wasn't the recruiter," I said.

"Well," he said. "There are better ways to pay off med school loans. We'll talk about it once you get closer to graduating."

We did. Talk about it. I am now sixty days from graduating. Mama and Pop don't think going into medicine will be good for me. They think I should be a forest ranger. I have no idea why, especially on days like today when my scalpel knows just where to go. Especially on days like today when I don't even have to refer to the drawing to locate the heart, the stomach, the liver, the urinary bladder.

Mama tells me that being a forest ranger will be quiet.

That I will be safe.

She says, "Trees help us breathe, you know."

○ ● ○ ○ ○

This morning, the school administration got a letter. The letter claimed to be from a student who was going to blow us all up before testing week. Nobody is supposed to know this, but I know. You want to know how I know, but I can't tell you that yet.

The point is: Somebody sent a letter and nobody knows who it was.

But I might.

He or she could be here with us today, scalpel in hand, and from here behind your plastic goggles you'd never know he or she could write that and send it.

He or she is not what you think.

I don't think they ever are.

Stanzi—Thursday— Formaldehyde

My frog is a contradiction—splayed out like a victim of violent crime. Left for dead. One of many. The frog also looks peaceful. If a frog can look proud, then mine looks proud. If a frog can look the opposite of proud, then mine looks like that, too.

I'm like this.

Cut in two.

Divided.

And so is the kid who sent that letter to the administration. Proud and humiliated at the same time. Splayed and standing at attention. Dead and utterly alive. Split right down the middle, neck to groin.

One freshman kid passed out so far. He joined the two conscientious objectors in the adjacent lab with the door closed so the smell of formaldehyde won't make them puke.

I like the smell of formaldehyde.

It preserves things.

What's not to like about something that preserves things?

Stanzi—Thursday— Tetra-gam-EE-tic Ky-MEER-a

Do you know what a tetragametic chimera is?

We learned about it during a genetics discussion last fall.

It's some crazy thing that happens to you between when you're conceived as cells and when you're a zygote. Somewhere between sperm-meets-egg and embryo. Somewhere between the one-night stand and the trip to the drugstore for the test kit. Somewhere in there you used to be fraternal twins. And you blended. Two into one.

It is not murder or homicide. Even though there were two and now there is one, you are only cells. Even though one of you is missing—really none of you is missing. You are all there. All two of you. But not at all two of you.

You belong this way.

Only no one knows it except your DNA. And nobody goes around looking at DNA—not unless they need to. Most tetragametic chimeras never know they're tetragametic chimeras. Except you have to know, right? You have to *feel* that somewhere. That twoness. The split. The schism.

I feel it.

I'm part leader and part follower. I'm part good and part evil. Part complicated, part simple. A human yin-yang. Where are you going? Where am I going? Why are you following me? Why am I following you? Why are we doing any of this?

Test week makes me ask questions. It splits me in two just as much as it always did. Last year they made me do makeup exams because the first time around, I filled the dots in according to how I was feeling when I read the question. A = Annoyed. B = Bored. C = Choleric. D = Disappointed. E = Empty. When I was done with makeup exams, I broke all my number two pencils in half so they could feel how I feel every day.

○○●○○

I've dissected so many things—from eggs to a bull's eye to a mouse, a snake, and a bird. Small animals seem easier to me. Once I hit senior AP biology, my emotions kicked in or something. Or maybe it was the summer trip to Columbine High School that lingered. I don't know. The larger animals seemed...different.

A fetal pig. I thought I would draw the line there. I thought I'd be grossed out dissecting a fetal pig. I thought about where we got it. Where did we get it? Where does one even get a fetal pig?

A cat. I *knew* I'd draw the line there. I couldn't cut open a cat. I have a cat. I feed it. I try to keep it alive with water and food, and I bought it a scratching post.

But I'd cut open a cat.

The scalpel didn't know it was a cat. The scalpel did what I told it to do. My hands—my hands are not mine some days. They belong to the other DNA. They are my twin's hands. They're capable of cutting open a cat and removing its liver. I'm not capable of doing that.

○●○○○

After frog dissection #7, I go to the library and do my homework. I'm the only one there. It's as if the bomb has finally exploded and I am the only survivor.

Then I go home and cuddle my living cat and watch *M*A*S*H*. I watch three episodes before I go to bed. The last one is "Love Story," season one, episode fourteen. Hawkeye Pierce says, *Without love, what are we worth? Eighty-nine cents. Eighty-nine cents' worth of chemicals walking around lonely.*

I think of what love must feel like. I'm not sure I know. I look at my cat. I ask it Hawkeye's question: *Without love, what are we worth?*

●○○○○

Did you know that the liver is the only organ that can regenerate itself? I bet Hawkeye Pierce knows this. I know Mr. Bio knows. I think Gustav knows, but because he might not, I turn off the TV and go out the back door toward his house. It's late, but I know where he'll be. He's always there. He's focused on one thing only ... and it's not me.

Half of me is okay with this. The other half is not okay with this. Half of me would follow Gustav anywhere. Half of me would lead. For now I want to tell him about livers.

Stanzi—Thursday Night— Livers

As I walk, I feel the rift in my cells. I don't know if everyone can feel their cells. I can feel every one of mine.

China says she can feel her cells. China is my best friend. China is inside out, so I bet she knows more about her cells than anyone.

Gustav doesn't care about cells. Gustav understands physics. He likes electrical engineering. He's building a helicopter.

Halfway to Gustav's house, a man steps out from behind a bush and asks me if I want to buy an *H*. I say I do not. "I don't need an *H*," I say.

"How about a *K*?" he asks.

I keep walking. When he yells something and I look back, he has his trench coat open and it's almost dark, but I can see the details that tell me he is an animal.

There is very little room in the suburbs to build a

helicopter, but Gustav does it anyway. There is very little room in my heart for Gustav, but I let him in all the same. We watch the movie *Amadeus* together sometimes, and I know he feels like the main character, Wolfgang Amadeus Mozart, and I know I feel like Mozart's wife, Stanzi. Those nights when we watch *Amadeus* I don't get a lot of sleep. I always dream biology operas in my head. The dead frogs dance. The dead cats sing. The fetal pigs play a perfect show on tiny fetal violins. They curtsy when the emperor acknowledges them.

I wonder if Gustav dreams operas of helicopters. Rotors and motors and stick shifts and altitude meters.

I'm not even sure if Gustav sleeps.

○●○○○

"Hey," I say.

"Hey."

"What're you doing tonight?" I ask.

"Building my helicopter. Can't you see it?"

I can't see it. It's Thursday.

Sometimes when I look at Gustav, I can picture him twenty years from now with a wife and kids—all of them flying around in his helicopter. I write them letters. The whole family. I write them postcards from my parents' creepy trips.

Hi, Gustav and family! Hope you get this okay! I still think about you every time I see a helicopter. I saw one today as I stood in front of the WELCOME TO THE UNIVERSITY OF TEXAS *sign. Do you know that line from season one, episode fourteen of* M*A*S*H

15

where Hawkeye said "Without love, what are we worth? Eighty-nine cents. Eighty-nine cents' worth of chemicals walking around lonely"? It's my favorite line. I always wanted to know if that was true. Are we really only eighty-nine cents' worth of chemicals? Can you tell me that one day? I miss you. Love, Stanzi.

I never send the postcards. I keep them in a box.

They make me mad sometimes.

Maybe had we not joined as mere cells, my twin would have the guts to send them. Maybe she'd have the guts to see Gustav's helicopter the other six days of the week. Maybe she'd have the mettle to just kiss him on his chapped lips.

For now, she seems to only know how to cut apart cats and fetal pigs.

"Livers regenerate themselves," I say to Gustav, who is still standing there looking at me with a monkey wrench in his hand.

"Do you mind if I go back to work?" he asks. "I have to get under the chassis, and I can't hear you from there. Tell me more about livers tomorrow."

"Sure," I say.

I walk home again.

The man jumps out from the bush and asks me if I want to buy a letter *F* and I jump behind the bush with him and kiss him like I mean it. He tastes like sawdust.

I ask him for a letter.

"You have to pay me," he says.

"I just did."

I begin to walk away and he grabs me by the back of my

collar and yanks me back into the bush. I fight him, but then he hands me a finely sculpted letter *S* and thanks me.

"No one has kissed me like that since I moved back here," he says. "You're very good at it."

I walk home smiling, pretending like I kissed Gustav, and I hang the *S* on my bedroom wall. I think it's some sort of high-tech papier-mâché; it's blue like limestone, but not heavy enough to be a real rock. I look at it and say, "Stanzi, you are a good kisser." Fact is, the *S* reminds me that I didn't kiss Gustav because I'm too scared to kiss Gustav. I don't know what I'm scared of. I know I'm scared of everything.

I open a random spiral-bound notebook and I draw a human body and I chop it up with lines. Hands. Feet. Head. Heart. Nose. Eyes. Lips. I draw an arrow to each and label it. *Me* for me. *Her* for her.

She gets hands, lips, and nose. I get the rest.

Stanzi—Friday—Juglone

We had another bomb threat today. This time it was sent with a present. Someone mailed a box to the superintendent and included two things: a hex nut from a helicopter kit and a dehydrated frog liver.

During AP bio, an administrative safety message is broadcast. Mr. Bio is supposed to lock down the area with a new red button they installed so no one can get into the science wing. He tells us we are supposed to hide in the back corner of the room and/or flee through the back lab in case of an intruder, depending on the situation.

There is nowhere to hide from a bomb, though.

Bombs are bigger than an intruder.

So we are calmly escorted outside after the recorded message is over.

During the bomb drill, I see Gustav talking to Lansdale

Cruise, the girl with the inexplicable hair. I read their lips. Lansdale says, "Hi, Gustav, still building your helicopter?" And Gustav answers, "Yes, I am." Lansdale asks, "Can I get a ride in it when you're done?" And Gustav walks away and stands by himself under the black walnut tree.

Juglone is the name of the poison produced by black walnut trees. Gustav says it kills everything that tries to grow under it except grass and resilient weeds.

I think Gustav and I are resilient weeds.

Stanzi—Monday—
A Man with a French Accent

It's Monday and I got off at Gustav's bus stop because I felt like it. I still can't see the helicopter, but I try anyway by squinting at the empty space inside his garage.

"Mortality doesn't scare me," Gustav says. "Living scares me. People are like insects." When I don't answer, he continues. "Hive mentality. They don't challenge themselves. They don't want to learn pi or build a house from scratch or do anything different. Who wants to live like that?" Gustav scratches his balls as if I'm not standing right here. "Insects," he says.

I want to say something about him scratching his balls, but I don't know if that makes me an insect or not. I don't want him to notice how wet I am from the rain and how dumb I look standing here in my lab coat, dripping. So I ask, "How can mortality not scare you? Isn't it sad that we're all going to die?"

"Not really," he says.

"Have you ever been to a funeral?" I ask him.

"Nope."

I think Gustav is spoiled.

He looks impatient for me to leave so he can go to work, and I do, without even a good-bye. I just walk toward my house in the rain with no umbrella.

When I pass by the bush, the man isn't there selling any letters. He only works that bush at night. During the day he works at the kitchen factory making cabinets. I see him drive there some mornings on my way to school.

I think about what Gustav said about dying. I'm scared to die. I'm only seventeen. I think I have something to do in the world, but I don't know what yet. I just think I deserve a chance to find out or something. A chance to test my DNA and see if I'm right about her—about me—about us—about the split. I want a chance to do more than what I do now.

When I get home, I strip off my wet clothes at the back door, hang up my lab coat so it won't get wrinkled, and have a bath while staring out the window into the limbs of the big maple tree in our backyard. We have a new bathtub— the fiberglass kind. When I take baths, I wish we had an old bathtub—the claw-foot kind. Iron. A tub that would make me feel safe in case anyone drives by shooting or blows something up.

I've been thinking about things blowing up since I was in fourth grade. I used to want to wear my bike helmet all the time. I wanted an army helmet like they have on *M*A*S*H*. Except blowing up isn't always external. It's not always easy to hear or see. Synapses fire every day in my brain. Thinking is just like exploding until it eventually scars you and you can't interact with people anymore. It's like one big, final detonation.

Gustav's is coming any day now. Mine, too.

The man who sells letters from behind the bush blows up every single night.

Kaboom.

Can't you hear the ticking?

I look around the bathroom as I soak in the bath and my skin turns pink. My book from last Christmas is still sitting, unread, on the back of the toilet cistern. It's called *Dealing with People You Can't Stand*. Mama and Pop said they bought it because it would help me deal with people I can't stand. They don't seem to know that they are the problem.

I'm the spawn of insects. I'm in love with Gustav, and he is also the spawn of insects. And I know the helicopter is there, but six days out of seven, I just have to trust.

A bomb threat was called in today and it was spoken by a man with a French accent. No one else knows this but me. Gustav knows, too, because I told him on the bus home. I think it's interesting about the accent. I figure if I have to be blown up, maybe it will be better being blown up by someone more interesting than just some weirdo American.

Gustav told me on the bus, "If I met the French-accent man on the street, I'd shoot him."

I said, "But what if you don't have a gun?"

He said he'd kill him with his bare hands.

Gustav is a pacifist. Gustav wouldn't even kill a mouse if it was eating his dinner right off his plate. He saw me think this internally and defended himself. "If it was a matter of life and death," he said, "I'd kill the French bastard."

"I don't think he was really French," I said.

"How do you know?" he asked.

"I just do," I said. That seemed to be enough to get him to stop asking.

I go back to looking at my pink bath-skin. I see the scar—the one on my thigh that's turned dark purple in the bath—and it tries to ask me a question but I drown it in the water and go back to looking out the window at the maple tree. I think about how there has to be a safer place to go without having to become a forest ranger. I think about Mr. Man-with-a-Gun who patrols our school. The police car always outside. They treat us like all we have is a skinned knee and we're bawling about how it stings.

A police-car-shaped Band-Aid.

A Mr.-Man-with-a-Gun-shaped Band-Aid.

And still, the bomb threats come in every day, sometimes twice a day. So many that the school might need a new phone to handle them all. So many that they might need to hire a bomb-threat secretary.

Maybe Gustav is right.

Maybe mortality is nothing to be afraid of.

Maybe the insects have won.

○ ● ○ ○ ○

I see three coffins in my head when I sleep.

Me, Gustav, and Adolf Hitler.

My coffin is white. Gustav's is red, like his helicopter. Adolf Hitler's is black and empty. While Gustav and I lie dead, Adolf dances in lederhosen that are too small for him. He is covered in beetles. As he dances, he becomes a beetle with giant legs. He begins to eat all the beetles he can see. His own friends. His own species.

He turns to Gustav and me and looks disappointed.

We could have been so much more, but no one would let us fly.

China Knowles—Tuesday Morning— I'm Fine

I am China—the girl who swallowed herself. I just opened my mouth one day and wrapped it around my ears and the rest of me. Now I live inside myself. I can knock on my rib cage when it's time to go to bed. I can squeeze my own heart. When I fart, no one else can smell it.

I write poems.

They look like those Salvador Dalí paintings I saw in the Philadelphia Museum of Art.

The Persistence of the Girl Who Swallowed Herself

Mouth forever too full to talk.
I saw inside everything
The whole world, a tiny galaxy, each cell of us.
I saw the universe.

I learned in English class about surrealists. It was the first time I wanted to throw myself up so I could be marked present. Surrealism turns the whole world upside down.

Upside down, everything makes sense. Upside down nothing will blow up and no one will hurt me for being in the wrong place at the wrong time and no one will pretend I'm not here or make me trust them when I shouldn't.

Anyway, I can't throw myself up. Swallowing oneself is not easy to undo. Not even for roller-skating. Not even for one of Lansdale Cruise's triple-cheese quiches.

It's like jail but noisier and quieter at the same time.

I don't need any bars. I don't need any guards. I don't even need a case file.

I'm fine.

I just swallowed one day and now I'm digesting. Constantly digesting.

Since the day I swallowed myself, I haven't been in any trouble. I quit smoking. I don't kiss any more boys. I got away from my skanky friends and I don't log on to the Internet. It's probably the best thing I ever did for myself apart from that time I ran from Irenic Brown last summer. But that's another story, and girls who swallow themselves can't tell stories. But I ran fast. I ran so, so fast.

The world is upside down unless I can find a way to turn myself right side out. Unless I can go back in time and stop the madmen.

How does an inside-out girl go about stopping all the madmen?

How does an inside-out girl go about turning back time?

○○○○●

I see Gustav on Tuesday morning during the bomb drill. He's talking to Stanzi, my best friend, the girl who always wears her biology lab coat, even when she's on the bus or at lunch. I always thought she was fat, but now I see she's just big-boned. Before I swallowed myself I was a lot more judgmental.

Now I have more time to think.

I stand on my own and stare at the brick building. One hundred and twelve days in a row. I wish they'd just do it. I'm ready. Gustav told me in physics class yesterday that he's not afraid to die. I thought about it all day. I think he's bullshitting.

Gustav once wore snowshoes for a week because he learned about string theory and didn't trust the molecular makeup of matter, and he says he's not afraid to die? How can he think he's fooling anyone? Everyone is afraid to die.

Stanzi—Tuesday at China's House

We stop by Gustav's on our way to China's house. Gustav always seems so much happier on Tuesdays. He asks, "It's really getting there, isn't it?"

I answer, "Wow, Gustav, you did so much in a week." I run my hand over the red fiberglass and it feels like satisfaction. It feels like something *real*.

As we walk to her house, China writes three poems about things that are real, and she hands them to me because sometimes she can't read aloud because she swallowed her mouth with her own mouth. When we get to China's basement, I read them for the three of us: Lansdale Cruise, China, and myself.

I say, " 'How to Tell if Your Quiche Is Real.' "

How to Tell If Your Quiche Is Real

We ate quiche that night
Spinach quiche

like the taste of bad dirt
like a sky full of bird shit.
Bitter like getting fired
even though you did your job
competently.
The quiche is real if it tastes good
with applesauce.
That night, the quiche
was dead.

How to Tell If Your Bed Is Real

Your bed is real if you are safe inside of it.
Your bed is real if you are safe outside of it.

How to Tell If Your Helicopter Is Real

If someone can see it every day,
then there's a good chance your
helicopter is real.
You don't ever have to see it yourself.
A matter of faith.
A matter of altitude.
Your helicopter is real if
when you fly it,
the screaming stops.

China's parents are into something weird. They have a table in
their basement that has binding on it. Eye hooks. Places to tie

and handcuff. They own whips and crops. They do not own horses.

We try not to think about it as we occupy the other half of the basement and sit in a cloud of awkward silence.

China and I sit there while Lansdale plays with her hair and talks about what it's like to have sex.

"It's really good most times," she says. "Except when the guy smells bad. Or if he doesn't know what he's doing." When China and I don't say anything, she continues. "I mean, some of them don't know what to *really* do, but they're all right."

China and I went onto a porn site once.

It was so dumb we were bored in under three minutes.

Then we watched a YouTube video about how to build self-esteem in cats.

China wrote this poem later that night.

Your Cat Has More Self-Esteem Than I Do

There are no billboards for cats
advertising feline plastic surgery
feline acne gels
feline gastric bands
feline face-lifts.
There are no commercials about
feline makeup
feline sex toys
feline fashion.
There are porn movies with cats,
but no cats watch them.

○●○○○

After Lansdale leaves, China tells me I should write poetry so I don't become a boring scientist like Gustav—lacking humor, concerned with only one thing. She says, "The most successful people in history used both sides of their brains."

I tell her I'm struggling with a poem I have to write for English class.

"You have to show it to me," she says.

"If I ever manage to write it, I will," I say. "And Gustav doesn't lack humor. He's very funny. You just have to get to know him better."

She says, "You're probably right."

As I walk home, the man jumps out from behind the bush. I let him sell me a glittery letter *R*. I only leave his bush lair once I straighten myself out. The *R* is a recycled lunch box, so I open and close it as I walk away. I leave a trail of red glitter like bread crumbs to home.

It's past eight o'clock. Mama and Pop have left me a note. It says, *Gone to bed. TV dinner in freezer. Make sure you turn out the lights.*

I don't know why they continue to write this note. They could just reuse the one they've written me every night since I can remember. I have too much homework to watch *M*A*S*H* yet, so I settle down at the kitchen table and I face it. I get to the worksheet Mr. Bio gave us today about our families.

Fill in the blanks.

Hair and eye color of your parents. Hair and eye color of

your grandparents. Hair and eye color of your siblings. The second half of the page asks for medical information. History of cancer? History of heart disease? History of autoimmune disease? History of dying from exploding bombs in school?

There are no questions on the bio worksheet about whether my parents like to visit sites of school shootings. There are no questions about how they take along Ziploc bags of saltine crackers with peanut butter and strawberry jam squished between so the jelly squirms out the tiny holes. No questions about how they picnic in empty, devastated parking lots with the windows rolled down.

There are no questions about being split in two all the time. No questions about my conflicting DNA. No questions about Gustav's helicopter or where he's going in it. No questions about the man in the bush who sells letters. No questions about why China swallowed herself or why Lansdale has such impossibly long hair even when she cuts it nearly every day.

Worksheets like this are boring to me. I'm into bigger things now. I'm making a groundbreaking discovery, only I can't tell anyone yet. I will one day discover an organ that no one ever told us about. Within that unknown part of us lies the cure for guilt. Maybe we can remove it or just touch it the right way, the way acupuncturists stab points and remove headaches. I can't explain it to you yet, but I know it's in there somewhere. I can't really test my theory on frogs or cats or anything because they don't have feelings, so it will take a human control group. I've been thinking I can test it on China and

Lansdale, but China is inside out and Lansdale doesn't seem to be guilty about anything.

I fill out the worksheet the best I can, and then I pull out a blank postcard from Greencastle, Pennsylvania. Greencastle was the site of the Enoch Brown school massacre in 1764. This massacre was brought to you by Pontiac's War, the rebellion against settlers by Native American tribes in this area of the United States.

I turn the postcard over and write to Gustav.

Dear Gustav, In case you were wondering, I'm glad you married a woman who can see your helicopter on all seven days. I think you deserve that kind of woman. She must be very brave. Love, Stanzi.

●○○○○

Truth is, my name isn't Stanzi. I only call myself Stanzi after watching the movie *Amadeus* too many times with Gustav. Truth is, my name doesn't really matter. I'm a character in a movie. In your book. In your mind. I play tug-of-war. I am a coward and a soldier. I am a pacifist and a warmonger. I am behind the bush with the man who sells letters, and I tell him secrets about who sends bomb threats to our school every day.

So, Stanzi is a pretty name but it's not mine. Constanze Mozart was a braver woman than I am. She was a braver woman than you are, too, if you're a woman. If not, she was a braver man.

I dare you to go back to 1779 and be seventeen years old.

You would be searching for light switches and toilets. You'd kill for a thermostat. A refrigerator. A telephone. You would pray for at least a 50% survival rate for your babies, and when you were blessed with one who lived through infancy, I bet you would do more than standardize it with tests or plop it in front of the TV.

We are polka-dotted with fungus. We are striped with bacteria. We are all so contaminated we are headed for the looney tunes.

Even choice picks like Gustav and China and me. Even Lansdale, with her talent for going into the bush man's lair and coming out with a letter at no cost to her. We are the very best you have to offer. Smart. Resilient. Dedicated. Competent.

And Gustav once wore snowshoes so he wouldn't fuse into the earth. And China has swallowed herself. And Lansdale has lied her hair long. And I am two people shoved into one. None of us will survive.

Stanzi—Wednesday—
We're Very Lucky

AP physics class will be held under the black walnut tree from now on. The spring weather has everyone in T-shirts and better emotional disposition. "At least this way, we can get something done," Gustav says. "At least this way, we aren't always in a state of drill. In. Out. In. Out. In. Out. Sniffed by dogs."

AP bio students make a circle next to a nearby holly bush and talk about our ancestors' hair and eye color. I didn't have time this morning to ask Mama and Pop about the family medical history, but I'm pretty sure they would have lied to me about it anyway.

Mr. Bio asks me which traits in my family are most common and I say, "Brown eyes and dark brown hair."

He nods and moves on to the other students. I don't listen. Instead, I watch a bird deep in the holly bush, calling out.

Surrounded by us. Trapped. Calling out for help, perhaps. Calling out in fear. Calling out about spring.

Good-bye, cold and snow!

Good-bye, hunger!

I look over to the black walnut tree. Gustav is talking to Lansdale Cruise again. Her hair hangs down to below her knees, and she fiddles with it as if it's a magician's medallion. She swings it and hypnotizes everyone. All of us, under a spell.

Lansdale has a reputation. When she talks about sex, we know she's never had it. When she gets letters from the bush man, we know she lied somehow to attain them. She is like Pinocchio except her hair grows, not her nose. A mixed-up fairy tale. Pinocchapunzel. I guess she's beautiful if you think beautiful people lie that much.

I note that Gustav looks uncomfortable talking to Lansdale. He looks past her. He looks at me. I can see inside his brain and this is what it looks like:

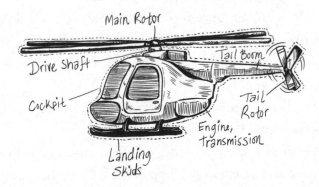

I asked him once where he's going to go in the helicopter. He told me he couldn't tell me yet, but I knew from his eyes that there is a destination. When I see him trying to talk to Lansdale, I wonder if he pictures the place in his head every day as he builds. I wonder if it's so far away that I might never see him again.

When AP-bio-at-the-holly-bush is over, I'm approached by the principal. She asks me to follow her back into the building. She sits me in a blue upholstered chair in her cluttered wood-paneled office and asks me to wait until someone else arrives.

I guess who someone else could be. *My parents, the guidance counselor, Mr. Bio, Gustav, China, Lansdale?*

I guess maybe she's found out about the man in the bush. Maybe she wants me to testify against him, though he's never done anything wrong to me. Then I guess I'm being too negative, and since it's spring, maybe I won a scholarship or something. I applied for two.

The principal returns with the superintendent.

I smile at them both as they close the door and sit down. They ask me, "Do you know who's sending these bomb threats?"

I answer, "Yes and no."

They say, "Don't be coy."

I say, "I'm not being coy. I don't want to speculate."

The principal says, "Didn't you dissect a frog last week?"

I say, "Yes. Many of us did."

The superintendent opens a box. It contains about five

frog livers, dehydrated. It also contains lug nuts, a condom still in its wrapper, a small bottle of red food coloring, a lock of Lansdale's long, lying hair, and a hinge from a saxophone key.

I don't know what to say, so I say, "That's an interesting boxful of things."

She says, holding up a frog's liver, "Do you know what this is?"

I say, "Did you know that the liver is the only organ that can regenerate itself? Isn't that amazing?"

The principal frowns. "Are those *your* frog livers?"

I say, "I don't have any frog livers, to my knowledge."

We all look at each other. The superintendent looks tired. She has black rings around her eyes. I wonder if she's slept since the bomb threats started.

She says, "Are you sure you don't know?"

I say, "I'm sure that I'm not sure. But I can keep trying to figure it out for you. I've been investigating since the first one. I'm close, but I can't be certain."

She nods.

"Did you get any fingerprints from the bomb-threat boxes?" I ask. "Or the letters?"

"No."

"Did you get traceable IP addresses from the bomb-threat e-mails?"

"No."

"Could the police trace the bomb-threat phone calls to any single number?"

"No."

"Looks like we are dealing with a very smart person," I say.

They stare at me.

Maybe they think I'm smart enough to do all these things. I'm flattered.

○●○○○

That night at home, Mama is there in place of the *Gone to bed* note because Pop has a late eye doctor appointment. While she takes a nap before dinner, I watch an episode of *M*A*S*H* where an unexploded bomb lands in the middle of the 4077th hospital compound. Hawkeye Pierce has to try to defuse it. It's high drama, but in the end it's just a bunch of funny flyers about the Army/Navy football game that explode into the sky.

A joke bomb. Just like ours.

I wonder what our joke-bomb letters would say.

English 12 . . . . .A
Calculus . . . . .B+
AP Biology . . . . .A
AP World History . . . . .B+
Physical Education . . . . . . .C-
Dear Mr. & Mrs. _____, Your son/daughter has been selected to serve as a square of human confetti in the science wing one day this year. Please sign this permission slip and return by tomorrow. Our condolences.

○○●○○

While we make enchiladas and line them up in the glass dish, Mama asks me how the drill was today. "Nice day to be outside," she says. "Spring has definitely sprung."

"I watched a bird in a holly bush," I say.

"What kind of bird?" she asks.

"*Eremophila alpestris*," I say.

She pretends I've said nothing.

"A horned lark," I say.

"Well, that's nice," she says, but she's already fastened into the TV news playing on the kitchen set. Something about a man who kept teenaged girls locked up in his basement for ten years. She's swallowed by the story, even though she knows all about it already. They've been looping it for days.

"The superintendent thinks I'm the one sending the bomb threats," I say.

"That's ridiculous," she says, not taking her eyes off the screen. "Of course it's not you."

"Of course," I say. "Or it could be. Nobody knows," I add, just to see if she's listening.

"How's Gustav?" she asks.

"I'm going to see him after dinner," I say. "But I have to finish my bio worksheet first. Can you tell me if we have any history of cancer, heart disease, or autoimmune disease in our family, and if so, who had it?"

She lowers her brow to think, then cocks her head toward me and claims we are a 100% perfectly healthy family that has never had any diseases.

40

"If more people were like us, then there'd be no need for health insurance!" she says. "If more people were as lucky as us, then the world wouldn't be so crazy!" she says.

"Yes," I say. "We're very lucky."

When I fill in the bio paper, I write that my maternal grandmother had cancer and my paternal grandmother has high blood pressure. I say that Pop's father is fighting dementia right now and that Mama's father has struggled with multiple sclerosis for the last five years.

When Pop gets home, we eat dinner together. It's a welcome break from the TV dinners I feed myself most nights. I tell Mama and Pop I can't seem to write my poem for English class. I tell them I still haven't heard back about the scholarships. I tell them I got an A on my statistics project.

Mama says, still watching the set with the sound muted, "Isn't it awful what that man did to those girls?"

Stanzi—Thursday—
That Soon

I can't see Gustav's helicopter, but because I saw it Tuesday, I comment on the tail propeller and how nice it looks.

"That's a rotor," Gustav says. "It's so we can steer."

I want to ask what he means when he uses the word *we*, but I know he must mean someone else. The woman I'm happy for him to marry. The one I write postcards to.

"I know it seems dumb," I say. "But I really do love the color. So bright!"

"They had the kit in black, too, but I chose red," he says.

"I'm glad."

Gustav smiles at me. "Do you ever take off your lab coat?" he asks.

"Not really," I say.

"Why not?" he asks.

"I don't know," I say. "Probably the same reason you wore your snowshoes that time."

"Aren't you hot, though?" he asks. He's wearing a T-shirt and a pair of shorts. The garage where he's assembling the helicopter is hot without a doubt, but I'm too shy to take off my lab coat, so I don't answer. I just shake my head.

He says, "Tomorrow I'll finish the engine and place it inside the chassis." He says, "We'll be flying in another week or so."

"That soon?"

"That soon."

"Why do you keep saying *we*?" I ask.

Gustav looks hurt. "Because you're coming with me, aren't you?"

I smile.

Gustav smiles.

"Are you sure you don't want Lansdale to come?" I ask.

"Lansdale lies too much," he says. "She serves no purpose."

"What about China?" I ask.

"China has eaten herself," he says.

"One of your physics friends?" I say. "Wouldn't they be a better copilot than me?"

"None of them believe," he says.

I tell him I'm honored and say I have to go home now. By the time I walk out, I'm sweating through my lab coat because I'm nervous and the garage is so hot. As I walk home, I wonder how we'll fly in a helicopter I can only see on Tuesdays. I wonder where we'll go. I wonder if we'll ever come back.

I wonder so much I forget about the dangerous bush until I'm several steps past it on the wrong side of the road. The bush man calls to me, so I cross and say hello.

I say, "Can you tell me where Gustav is going in his helicopter?"

He looks disappointed. "Don't you want it to be a surprise?"

"I don't like surprises," I say.

"Well," he says, "I can't tell you. That's up to him."

"Have you ever loved somebody?" I ask him.

"Yes."

"Does it always hurt so much?" I ask.

"When does it hurt?" he asks.

"All the time."

"I'm not sure that's love," he says. "You may be sick."

"My mother is Hawkeye Pierce. He says without love we're just eighty-nine cents' worth of chemicals walking around lonely."

"He's probably right," the bush man says.

He gives me a stuffed purple velvet lowercase *f* for my trouble, but I drop it at his feet and walk home feeling like eighty-nine cents of chemicals.

My bedtime story is season one, episode twenty-three, "Ceasefire." Everyone at the M*A*S*H 4077th hospital believes a rumor of a cease-fire, but there really isn't one. I go to bed knowing how they feel.

China Knowles—Thursday— It's True

I am China and I have swallowed myself and your brother, too. Last week I swallowed a little girl who didn't know where her mother was. Tomorrow I will swallow a teacher who forgets how to teach. I don't just swallow myself. I swallow anyone who's willing. It keeps me from being lonely in here.

There is a girl who sobs every day in the girls' bathroom next to the gym. I don't know why she sobs and I don't know who she is, but I hear her every day, sobbing. I go to that bathroom to sit down and think for a minute, and she goes there to sob. I've asked her if she would like me to swallow her, but she hasn't answered me yet. I believe she's thinking about it.

It's a big decision, to be swallowed.

Once you're swallowed, you can only be found by people

who understand guts. Once you're swallowed, the only way out is to push yourself back out.

I won't be crude about it, but you know what I mean.

Lansdale would say something like, "You need to take a colossal shit and find your head in there somewhere."

Stanzi would say something like, "It's actually impossible to swallow yourself, you know."

Stanzi has guts I wish I had. She always tells the truth. She can dissect any animal without fainting. She can walk by the man in the bush when the rest of us take the parallel road. She sends me postcards from where her parents take her on vacation and always signs them *Love, Stanzi*. I can't even write the word *love*. I can't even think about the word *love*. Not since Irenic Brown.

I'd bet all my father's money that Stanzi will fly out of here with Gustav when he finishes the helicopter. She says he'll take Lansdale, but I know it's her. He looks at her all the time when we're outside for the drills. Then, when she feels his stare and looks over at him, he looks somewhere else.

Irenic Brown was like that with me, too, before we started to go out. I used to think it was because we were meant to be, like Stanzi and Gustav. Turns out it was just a trick. It was all just a trick.

Some Boys Have Tricks

We believe them like
we believe the weatherman

when he predicts snow
and when he's wrong, we shrug
and blame ourselves for
ever believing him.

The night I ran, I ran all the way back to my house. Two miles. Two miles is a long way. Two miles is a long way to think. And yet, I only thought one thing for those two miles. I thought: *Run, run, run, run, run, run, run.*

When I got home and into the shower, I thought about other things. Pregnancy. Diseases. Lies. Tricks. What he'd said.

Why No One Will Believe You

You are a dumb weathergirl
who cries *Storm! Storm!*
Every time you speak
we take you less seriously.
When we whisper in your ear
we say
Even if it snows, you're full of shit.
Ask anyone.
You're untrustworthy.

AP English is the one class a day where I pay some sort of attention. I like the truth. I like expression. I like the feeling of yelling like Sylvia Plath or Walt Whitman. They yelled louder than any dumb voice, and they used paper, too.

They said more than I can ever say about the truth.

The truth is upside down.

Everything is upside down.

That's all that comes out when I try to explain why I swallowed myself.

I am a human being, but nobody seems to recognize this.

I think I'm becoming good friends with Lansdale Cruise. Before, I thought she was just like one of my old slutty friends. Oxymoron. I can't really call them my friends if I'm simultaneously calling them slutty, can I?

Lansdale Cruise isn't slutty at all. She lies to protect herself. She's a nerd, but the nerds don't like her. She's a popular girl, but the popular girls don't like her. She has a secret and she won't let me tell Stanzi. I find it hard to lie to Stanzi. We're best friends and Lansdale is new, but still, I have to keep a promise when I make it, and it's easy for a swallowed girl to keep secrets.

There Is Nothing Stupid About Home Economics

It's learning how
to be independent
to do your own wash
to cook your own food.
It's learning how to
budget so you don't end up
a dick with ten maxed
credit cards and a mortgage

you can't pay.
If the world explodes
as predicted
I'd want to be near
Lansdale Cruise.
She can balance
a checkbook.
A three-course meal.
She makes the best
red velvet cupcakes.

I am China—and today I can see Gustav's helicopter. It's a shade of red rivaled only by the color of my stomach, which is all anyone can see now. Gustav won't look at me, and I think it's because he knows.

It was on the Internet.

It was passed around like my parents pass around joints during their basement parties.

It wasn't just some rumor. It was viral.

I ask Gustav how soon he thinks the helicopter will fly. He says a week or two. I tell him we still have fifty-six days of school left. He sneers and says, "What school? You mean the drills? The dogs? Test week? That's not school."

When I try to apologize for pissing him off, he adds, "I've learned more in this garage in the last nine months. Haven't you, China? Haven't you learned more outside school than in it?"

This is how they act   all of them—the people who know.

And everyone knows. Why would anyone respect *that girl*? I remember when it happened to Tamaqua de la Cortez. I called her a slut myself. When they all called her a stupid spic who deserved everything she got, I nodded my head.

You know what I wanted?

Silence.

And look what I got.

Silence.

I walk out of Gustav's garage and head home. I take the road with the dangerous bush. When the man steps out, I punch him right in the teeth and he falls backward into his green dungeon. I don't run. I walk and I shake the pain out of my fist. He doesn't follow me.

Did you know they don't like girls who fight back? That they usually give up on us? They've done studies. It's true.

Except sometimes it's not.

Lansdale Cruise—Friday— It's a Party

Fridays suck.

Fridays are the bridge to the weekend, when I'm hit with frying pans, croquet mallets, my mother's favorite fish slice. I'm scorched with cigarettes.

Sometimes, they sever the soft skin between my toes and rub table salt in.

But not really. They could only do that stuff if they were home.

Mr. and Mrs. Cruise are never home on weekends.

So no one is there to beat me except me.

I had a job once in the kitchen boutique and that kept me busy, but then a guy came in one day and robbed us and I got shot, so now I sit in my panic room all weekend until my parents come home. The only friend I have in the world is my Doberman, Crunchy.

Except I don't have a dog or a panic room and I never had a job.

I can't stop myself.

I'm melting from the ennui of being the most normal girl in the world. If I had guts, I'd go to college parties and drink vodka, like China used to. She's gutsy. She swallowed herself and now she's a walking digestive tract. She digests on paper and we can see what she ate that day.

Usually she eats the past.

She's especially afraid of the bomb dogs in school. They roam around with their trainers and they do their job. They sniff. They sniff for nothing because there is a difference between a threat and a bomb.

A bomb is something people make out of chemicals. A threat is something we all have, like snot or eye boogers or something. It's a human body part.

Threat (n.) 1. *part of a student that makes them so scared they spend all day in their room on the weekends.* 2. *part of a student that makes them tell lies so people will like them because somewhere else inside their body is a panic button that never stops getting pressed.*

Our first intruder drill was last year. I was a junior. They told us to hide in closets. I did what they told me during the drills, knowing that if a real intruder came, I'd bail out the window before I'd trap myself in a closet. Didn't they ever watch a horror movie?

I hate Fridays because weekends are boring. It's exciting having bomb threats every day. It's something better to do. It's a distraction. It's a party. We have made it a routine, and it's a reason to get up in the morning.

I like seeing how people don't care anymore. I like hearing the other students getting sarcastic. *I wish they'd fuckin' blow it up already. I hope today's real, man; I didn't do my chem homework.*

Fridays suck because I lied about seeing Gustav's helicopter.

I say I can see it, but I can't.

I've tried every day of the week and I can't see a thing.

I use facts I hear from China and Stanzi and I know it's red and it's almost finished, so I can fake it pretty well. Most of all I twiddle my hair and pretend like I like Gustav, but he's not my type.

I'm looking for someone older.

Forty, at least. Someone who needs a good wife who knows how to do everything in a house. That's all I want. Imagine if I said that out loud. They'd burn me as a witch.

But it's true.

I want to be a wife, have babies, and make a man happy. And I want to be happy myself.

Until then, I live a lie and chop off a foot of hair a day so my stepmom doesn't notice and say something bitchy like, "I hate how you get more beautiful and I just get saggier and uglier."

I may be beautiful—if you believe in Barbie beauty—but I'm not like China, who can write down her feelings, or Stanzi, who can spit out logic like it's some kind of scientific burp or something. I don't have the bond they have. It's impossible to have a best friend if you move every two years because you're an irrational liar and people begin to hate you once they find out. All I have is Mr. and Mrs. Cruise, providers of a house and food in the refrigerator. Mrs. Cruise is not my mother.

My mother was two wives ago. Daddy likes them young.

Stanzi—Saturday—Waltzing

China is spending the day doing something with Tamaqua de
la Cortez.

Just because I'm in a lab coat and up to my eyes in dead
animal organs a lot of the time doesn't mean I didn't hear
about what happened to Tamaqua. Everyone heard.

China seems to think I heard something about her, too.
She says, "You know." She says, "Everyone knows." She said to
me yesterday morning at the drill, "Even Gustav knows."

She doesn't understand that I don't want to know. Not
about anything. I want to crawl into a hole and not come out.
I want to split in two so I have something to say. I want to go
somewhere where there are so many mirrors that there is a
reflection of twenty of me and I don't have to choose the one I
like best.

I keep having this dream.

There are four coffins standing upright. One is mine and one is Gustav's. The other two are nailed shut, and I don't have a crowbar.

Each coffin has a doorbell. I ring Gustav's twelve times and he answers wearing a tuxedo and top hat. He asks me if I know how to waltz and I feel stupid because I don't know how to waltz. He tells me it's okay because he doesn't know how to waltz, either.

Then the drill bell sounds and the other two coffins open and the entire student body pours out of them. There are twelve hundred teenagers crowding us, waltzing. They waltz beautifully. The song is Mozart's Waltz no. 1. It is played solely by cellos.

This is the waltz drill.

I realize in the dream that Gustav and I are failing the waltz drill.

We don't panic. We seem to enjoy the others' ability to waltz so well. We hold our hands to our mouths as if we are viewing something extraordinary. Then we go back to our coffins and close the doors.

Then we are in the helicopter, flying higher and higher.

The student body is below us, and as they waltz, they look like a thousand tiny test dots, changing their minds with each step.

A, B, C. A, B, C. A, B, C.

The music stops and they all turn into tiny beetles and scurry into their respective dots and stay there.

Then I wake up.

○●○○○

Mama and Pop say we're going for a short family outing tomorrow. They tell me it will be fun. I go onto my master list and try to figure out which crime scene they have in mind.

State College? Swarthmore? Edinboro?

I got the master list from a list of school shootings on the Internet encyclopedia. But sometimes they list people who just happened to shoot themselves/their lover/their enemy in a school. The list goes all the way back to Pontiac's War. It's like they added these not-really-school-shootings to the list to make it look like there have been school shootings all through history. You know, to downplay the problem or something.

Gustav is right. You can't read a thing or see a thing or study a thing without seeing the infestation. I walk to his house to tell him. Really, I should be writing my poem for English. It's due on Tuesday. I still haven't even tried. It's just a poem. I don't know why I'm so worked up about it.

○○○○●

The dangerous bush man has set up a lemonade stand. He is selling pink and classic lemonade. He has a sign that reads ROOFIES COST EXTRA. I stop and ask him how much the lemonade costs and he says, "A quarter." I ask him how much lemonade with the roofies cost and he says, "Add a dollar."

I ask him how business is.

He says, "Not a lot of people walk by here anymore."

Gustav is lying on the concrete on his back with a large pair of pliers and a screwdriver. Next to him on the garage floor are a welding torch and a face shield. I can smell burnt metal.

"Still in your lab coat?" he asks.

"Yep."

"Do you dissect things on weekends?" he asks.

"Do you build your helicopter on weekends?" I answer.

"Touché," he says. A minute flies by. "Do you want some lemonade?" He points to the pitcher of pink lemonade that sits on the tool bench next to the large garage door.

"Did you get that from the man in the bush?" I ask.

"Yes."

"Did you pay extra for the roofies?"

"Of course not," he says.

"I trust you."

"I know," he says. "You're probably the one who trusts me the most."

This makes me feel guilty because if I'm the one who trusts him the most, I should be able to see the helicopter all seven days.

"Can you tell me where we're going yet?" I ask.

"We're going to an invisible place," he answers without looking up from his work. "We're flying an invisible helicopter to an invisible place."

"Did you know the man in the bush knows where we're going?" I ask.

"Who do you think bought me the kit?"

I feel my forehead move into a frown—not a sad frown, but a thoughtful one. I say, "The bush man bought you the helicopter? You said it cost you, like, fifty thousand dollars."

Gustav doesn't answer.

"And did he tell you where you were going?"

"He told me that people like us—like you and me and him—that we don't belong here. We belong somewhere else."

"In the invisible place?"

"Yes," he answers. "Apparently, it's a hotbed of genius."

Half of me laughs at this. Half of me cries.

Stanzi—Saturday Night—
Amadeus

I watch Gustav build his helicopter until daylight disappears.

"You're a good friend to sit here with me all day watching me build something you can't even see," he says.

"I'm only here so we can watch *Amadeus* when you're done," I say. "I'm a selfish friend who doesn't own the movie herself." Mama and Pop don't like me watching sad things.

You must understand, *Amadeus* is the most tragic love story. It's a love story between the composer Wolfgang Mozart and his wife, Stanzi. It's a love story between Mozart and his disapproving father. It's a love story, most of all, between Mozart and his music. And it's tragic because it's a story of jealousy, waste, and the contempt for genius. It's tragic because nothing has changed, really.

Gustav is mocked for building a helicopter with his own hands. I want to stick up for him. *Shut up! Shut up! Can't you see he's a national treasure? Can't you see his light?*

They'll understand one day as we fly overhead. They'll be out on the athletic field enduring more drills. The administration will move the entire school outside once the weather warms. Desks, chairs, the poster of the periodic table of elements. They will vote to blow the school up as a prophylactic to bomb threats. They will vote for anything so long as they don't have to find out why it's happening.

Gustav finishes a twelve-hour Saturday of work and stops in the bathroom to wash the grease off his hands. The grease is never invisible. He walks to the kitchen, which is behind the sunken den where we will watch *Amadeus*. I follow him and keep my hands in the pockets of my lab coat.

"I'm going to make popcorn," Gustav says. "Do you want more lemonade?"

"Sure."

"If I give you a quarter, will you go get some?"

I walk down the empty sidewalk and when I get to the lemonade stand, the bush man is still there. The sign now reads NO ROOFIES COSTS EXTRA. There is a small bit of impossibly long blond hair poking out from under his *Thuja orientalis* bush.

I ask him how much for no roofies.

"A hundred dollars," he answers.

I hand him what I have, a quarter, and I ask for a pitcher of pink lemonade with no roofies.

As he pours he says, "It's like a lottery, sweet cheeks. Do you trust me?"

"No."

"But you want the lemonade?"

"Yes."

"Well, good luck with this," he says, handing me the pitcher.

I don't know what to say to Gustav when I return. I want to warn him, but I don't want to sound like an alarmist.

I say nothing.

We set up the movie and Gustav brings popcorn with butter and a little bit of salt and we eat it from the same bowl and watch as Wolfgang Amadeus Mozart unfolds on the screen in front of us.

We watch as he plays for the emperor as a prodigy.

We watch as he meets Stanzi and tackles her and kisses her and I blush but Gustav can't see it because he is too busy eating popcorn and hiding the rise in his pants because Stanzi Mozart's breasts are fantastic in those 1700s dresses she wears.

We watch as Mozart is told his music has *too many notes*.

We watch as he is slowly psychologically poisoned by Antonio Salieri, a rival composer who is split in two like I am. He loves Mozart. He loves his talent. He knows Wolfgang is drenched with gift. But, oh, he hates him. He hates him for being so talented now. *Why now?* Why wasn't Mozart born *after* Salieri had his chance to shine? Why is he secretly known as the eccentric genius while Salieri maintains mediocrity?

Jealousy is the tragedy of this movie.

And I have been jealous.

And though Lansdale Cruise keeps her secrets from me, I can see in her eyes that she will have the perfect life while I remain obscure and big-boned.

Go ahead. Name me the scientists who've cured diseases. Name me the scientists who discovered the medications that may be helping you *right now as you read this*. You can't, can you? You can't name the titles of their published academic papers. You can't even tell me how they discovered what they discovered.

But I guarantee you can name me twenty talentless people who got famous for doing *nothing*.

That will be Lansdale Cruise.

And part of me isn't jealous about it. And part of me hates her already for it.

Part of me wants to brush her hair. Part of me wants to chop it all off in uneven stabs.

"Don't you like the lemonade?" Gustav asks.

"Not really," I say.

"Do you want something else?" he asks.

Then his father walks in and turns up the dimmer switch so we are both blinded by the den's recessed lighting.

"What are you two doing in here?" he asks. "Gustav, why aren't you reading the flight manuals I brought you yesterday?"

"I'm taking a break," Gustav says. "I'm seventeen. I do require breaks sometimes."

"Don't get snippy," Gustav's father says. Then he turns to me. "Hello, Stanzi," he says. "What are you watching?"

When we tell him, he rolls his eyes and says, "I don't know why you're wasting your time on that rot."

Gustav's father doesn't understand love.

Gustav's father doesn't understand biology.

Gustav's father kills his own daffodil bulbs by mowing them too early and doesn't care about whether they grow again next year or not. Gustav's father likes grass. In his eyes, watching *Amadeus* for two and a half hours is akin to letting clover and dandelions infest the whole lawn.

When he leaves, Gustav has to get up and dim the lights again. When he sits down next to me, he's closer. I can feel his hip. We balance the popcorn bowl in the valley made by our touching outer thighs.

The movie ends and dead Mozart is dumped into a common pauper's grave with a dusting of lime. Gustav presses the button on the remote to turn the TV off. We sit for a minute in the dimmed room and are silent. He moves the empty popcorn bowl from between us to the coffee table. He fidgets. If I were to guess what he's doing, I'd guess he's getting ready to kiss me.

I get up, straighten my lab coat down my hips. I say, "I'm going on a drive tomorrow with my parents. I'll see you at school Monday."

Everything freezes for a too-long second.

"Have a nice time," he says. "You're very lucky that your parents take you on so many trips."

I've never told Gustav where we go. He's never seen my snow globes. He's never received the postcards I never send him. He thinks we go to see elaborate gardens or state parks because that's where I tell him we go.

"Yes. I'm very lucky," I say.

"I'll be stuck here reading flight manuals."

"It's not so bad," I say. "Soon you'll know how to fly. That's really something, isn't it?"

"It is."

I want to ask him where we're really going in the helicopter, but I'm tired and I think this is a good place to leave the conversation.

As I walk down the road to my house, I walk on the other side of the street from the bush man's lair. I'm not in the mood. I don't want to see Lansdale if she's still there. When I pass, he pokes his head out and smiles. There is no blond hair. Just him. Naked again, I bet. I scowl at him from across the road.

As I near my house, half a block away, I hear him call out to me.

I can't help that the world is upside down! I can't do anything to change it!

Stanzi—Sunday—Red Lion

We drive to Red Lion, Pennsylvania.

We travel at warp speed back to 2003, when a fourteen-year-old kid shot his principal and then himself in front of hundreds of people. Mama reads an article aloud about the day it happened. She says that according to the US Department of Veterans Affairs, 77% of witnesses to a school shooting will end up with PTSD.

Post-traumatic stress disorder.

Seventy-seven percent.

Hawkeye Pierce from *M*A*S*H* would know this is bullshit. He's a doctor. He'd laugh, dressed in his red bathrobe on top of his olive drab, and he'd say something smart like, "What happens to the other twenty-three percent? Do they get eaten by bears?" He'd probably be a little drunk on homemade gin. He'd probably have a girl on his arm. A nurse. She'd laugh at his joke and say, "Oh, Hawkeye."

We get to the school in Red Lion and we can't go in, of course. All we can do is park in the empty Sunday parking lot. We stare at the building and Mama cries. Pop rubs her back. I do what I always do. I think about how I'm split down the middle. Part of me wants to blow up everything. Part of me searches for a needle big enough to stitch it all together again. I think Hawkeye Pierce felt like that, too.

Stanzi—Sunday—
The Answers

The dangerous bush man isn't selling lemonade tonight. He's not in the bush. I can't imagine where he'd be on a Sunday evening, but I guess everyone must need a day off and maybe today is his.

I walk into his bush and check to make sure. No man. No trench coat. No letters for sale. When I walk out of the bush, China is standing there, staring at me with her stomach. She is shivering—from fear, not cold. China never walks down this road. China always uses the parallel road because of the bush man.

"Is he in there?" she whispers.

"No."

"Oh," she says. She shakes even more. I can hear her teeth chattering somewhere inside herself.

"Are you okay?" I ask.

"I was coming to ask for...um...help with my homework."

"Why would he be able to help with your homework?"

"He has the answers," China says.

"Can I help?"

"No."

"Want to come to Gustav's with me?" I ask.

"I can't. I said I'd meet Lansdale with the answers."

"The answers?"

"For our...um...homework." China isn't looking directly at me. Not even with her duodenum.

"Are you sure everything's okay?" I ask.

She lets out a sigh. "That's what *he* always asks," she says, pointing to the bush.

I wait a minute to see if I'll eventually understand what she's talking about. Then I realize it's hard to understand what a stomach says. I think that's the point. It may be why China swallowed herself in the first place.

"Will we walk home together tomorrow?" I ask. "I'd love to hear some of your new poems."

"Have you finished your poem for English yet?" she says. "You can read it to us."

"I haven't had time," I lie. "I can't figure out what to write about."

"You should dissect something and think about it," she says. "Frogs always help you concentrate."

She scurries off then, in the direction of Lansdale's house.

She is off-balance, teetering. I wish I knew what to say to her these days, but I don't.

○●○○○

Gustav is suspended from a bungee screwed into the ceiling. He is hovering above the main rotor, I bet, securing the fixed ring at just the right angle. I've been reading up on helicopters. They aren't so different from frogs, really—just a bunch of parts that make a whole.

He's got his tool belt on, and it jingles as he rotates himself around on the bungee. I can see he is concentrating deeply, so I walk in, I sit on the upturned plastic five-gallon bucket, and I wait. Two hours go by. Gustav has sweat out a pitcher of pink lemonade, and his father brings him a protein bar and then drinks Gustav's sweat and replaces it with a bottle of water that Gustav gulps down in one go.

Gustav's father glares at me, the distraction, even though I haven't said a word.

After two hours of this, I wave good night and walk toward my house.

The dangerous bush man catches me off guard.

"Give this to China," he says as he hands me a long string of flat, colorful cardboard letters—like the kind on our HAPPY BIRTHDAY sign at home.

The letters go on forever. Infinity. I can't fit them all into my hands, so I let them trail behind me. They are the same letters. *A*, *B*, *C*, *D*, *E*. *A*, *B*, *C*, *D*, *E*. Just not in that order. As I walk home, the weight of infinite letters drags me and I leave them on my driveway where one of Mama's snotty tissues escaped her cleanup mission when we got back from Red Lion. I call China.

"The man from the bush gave me your answers," I say. "They're really long. Can you come and get them?"

She asks for my help.

I meet her three minutes later in the driveway and the two of us try to pull the string to her house, but infinity is too heavy.

"What did you have to do to get this many letters from him?" I ask.

"It was Lansdale," she says.

"Well, what did *she* have to do?"

"She never has to do anything. She's Lansdale," China answers.

We stop trying to pull the letters any farther. She calls Lansdale on her cell phone and they decide to dictate the answers. China will read them and Lansdale will write them down.

I hear Lansdale say, "Don't forget. You have to start at the beginning. If we get even one out of order, we're screwed."

I help China find the very beginning of the string of letters, and she reads. "A B E C D A B C A D D E A D A A B D C A D..."

I wave good night after I get a chair from the porch and place it under her. She sits and pulls the string of letters over her lap as if she's spinning wool, letter by letter.

I think about what can be woven from wool. Things as small as baby booties or a tiny hat for your pet hamster. Things as large as king-sized blankets. Tents. The world's longest scarf. I think about what can be woven from letters. Things as small as China's haiku or a tiny *I love you* note. Things as large as laws. Treaties. And during test week, one could knit a scarf that wraps around the equator a million times—all from those five letters.

China Knowles—Monday—
I Love You

I am China, the walking colon. I'm still not as full of shit as Lansdale is, but if you can overlook her knack for storytelling, she's all right.

And she's got a photographic memory, which makes her an ally.

Or a superhero. I can't figure out which.

She's helping me because she told me she heard everything from Irenic Brown's dumbass friends. She asked if Stanzi was any help to me and I didn't answer because Lansdale can't replace Stanzi. Lansdale can give me one kind of help. Stanzi has given me science.

Stanzi and I have counted the number of Irenic's girl-friends since me, and I watch them during the drills. There have been at least ten girlfriends. They look different now, too. None of them are internal organs on legs, though. Not that anyone can tell from the outside.

They all thought he loved them. I know that for sure. Tamaqua de la Cortez told me this is how it's done. He's always the first one to say *I love you*. He'd say it quickly. Suddenly. As if it slipped out in an embarrassing moment of sincere emotion.

I Love You

No girlfriend would
call the police
about it.
That's the best part.
You act confused.
She acts confused.
You do it.
Strong and deaf.
Like you can't hear
her saying no
please
stop.
Pin her down but
leave no mark.
She can't figure out
what you just did.
She can't figure out
if it's her fault
or your fault
or nobody's fault

and while she juggles
the answers
you slip out of her life
and tell her that it
wasn't
really
working.
If she wanted
she could go to the
hospital and they could
find you inside.
Up there.
In the dark.
But all you have
to say is
she was my girlfriend
and she's pissed I
broke up with her.

Lansdale comes up to me before homeroom. She hands me the stack of papers with the bush man's letters written on them.

"We're golden," she says.

I nod.

"Do you think Stanzi needs these, too?" she asks.

"Stanzi doesn't cheat," I say. She doesn't. Stanzi's guilt complex is far too large. It's bigger than Jupiter, and Jupiter is 43,441 miles in radius. It's something we have in common, only we never talk about it.

Lansdale shrugs and asks if I wrote any new poems. I show her this one:

Your Number Two Pencil Has More Self-Esteem Than I Do

They write your name and
date of birth in the rectangles
at the top of the page
and if your name doesn't fit
they will change it.

You are student number 202876.
Your scores indicate that
while you may worry about things
that happened in your past,
you are just fine.

"I don't even know what you're talking about half the time," Lansdale says. She stops to tie up a new, long strand of hair that only appeared since the last time I saw her. "But I still think you're cool."

I look through the stack of papers she gave me with the bush man's letters on them, and I don't know how I'm going to memorize these in three hours. She can memorize anything. It's how she maintains near normalcy while being a pathological liar.

"Don't worry," she says. "It's easy to remember this kind

of shit. Just make sentences out of them." She seems distracted and she pulls out another paper, hands it to me, and says, "Look what I found on the kitchen table this morning. My stepmom left it."

Complaint for Dissolution of Marriage

Since in or about 2014 until the
current time, defendant has
failed to offer
companionship
or affection as if in a healthy relationship.
Despite plaintiff's exertions in this regard,
defendant has
rejected
discussion about said issues with
plaintiff. Due to this
extreme
cruelty
toward the plaintiff, there is no
solution except to dissolve the marriage.

Lansdale looks a mix of angry and nonplussed. She says, "She used to tell us stories about her ex and how *cruel* he was. Now I know she was just full of shit."

Lansdale has to go to class. I give her the divorce paper, and when it's gone I feel the need to sanitize my hands in case it spreads.

Stanzi—Monday—I Want to Show You Something

During the first drill early Monday morning, China passes me a note: *I want to show you something. Follow me.* She is carrying a stack of papers with letters on them. She smells like hand sanitizer.

I follow her to a back door that has been propped open into the locked-down school and we go to her locker, where she tosses in the stack of papers and removes a stuffed backpack. She points to my locker and tells me we're not coming back today, so I put my books in and take out my purse and a few things.

She tells me to bring a book to read.

"Why do I need a book?"

When she doesn't answer, I grab the book I've been reading.

While we walk back to the door, we hear the sniffer

dog patrol. China tenses. I grab her wrist and take her down another set of steps and to a different exit door, and when we use it, the alarm sounds but nothing explodes from the building except two girls who blend into their throng of outdoor classmates until they can make a break toward the bus station.

"If we run, we can catch the nine thirty," China says.

When we get there, China buys us two tickets to New York City.

I worry for about a minute. I worry about all the stuff normal people worry about. But then I remember that I don't care. Who cares if I get detention in a school that's never open except to police and bomb dogs? Who cares if Mama and Pop get a phone call from the principal?

They think I'm a biology genius on her way to biology-genius college, and I am.

I take a bus schedule from the counter of the bus station, and once we find our seats on the bus, I check how long our ride will be—two and a half hours.

I watch the countryside go by. We pass flea markets that are closed on weekdays and a gun store that boasts THE LARG-EST SELLER OF MILITARY WEAPONS IN THE AREA! on a sign out front. I see two other kids skipping school behind a barn, smoking cigarettes and making a getaway plan. That's what we just did. That's what we do in the drills. We get away from what we're supposed to be doing.

China hands me a poem before we cross the New Jersey border.

Untitled

I met a boy on the Internet
and his name is Shane.
I'm sorry I didn't tell you
but you are so
out
of
reach
because I am so
out
of
reach.
You can see the helicopter.
And I lied.
I can't see it.
Never once have I seen it.
And I'm sorry for that, too.

○○○●○

I hop over into the seat next to China's seat.
    "Does Shane live in New York?" I ask.
    She nods.
    "Have you met him before?"
    She holds up two fingers. "Twice."
    "Is he cute?"
    She smiles. "Yes."
    "Did you tell Lansdale?"

She nods, then looks at her knees. "Yes. Sorry."

I attempt to read. But really, the whole time I'm thinking about Gustav.

Here's China, inside out, casually hopping a bus to New York City to see a boy she barely knows, and Gustav lives a four-minute walk from my house. I see him nearly every day, and still we can't admit we're in love because there are more important things. In his case, the helicopter. In my case, I'm not sure I can love anybody without screwing it up.

○●○○○

When we get to Port Authority in New York City, China weaves her way down into the subway. She has a MetroCard. She swipes it and walks through the turnstile and then she hands the card to me and I monkey what she just did and then I'm standing on the other side, the sound and smell of underground trains and grease and sparks and millions of people who walk through here every day.

It's just past noon on a Monday. All I know is that I have to be home by tomorrow to see Gustav's helicopter.

"Are we going back tonight?" I ask her.

She nods. "I just want to see him for an hour."

"I can't wait to meet him," I say.

"You can't," she says. "You can't see him."

I look at her. My eyes say, *Why did you bring me, then?*

"You can go to the museum," she answers. She hands me a pass to the museum.

The subway train letters are in colorful circles. A, C, E.

The subway train letters are just like answers, so I spend our quiet walk to the right track coming up with questions.

Will they notice us missing at school today?

A

Will our missing today's drills mean lower scores for the school? Less money for next year? Teachers fired?

C

Is that Mozart I hear?

E (flat major)

Two young men—our age, maybe a little older—are playing the Sinfonia Concertante in E-flat Major and they're so good, I steer myself to their open violin case and drop in a five-dollar bill.

I turn to China. "I don't want to go to a museum."

She tells me I can wait for her in the vegan juice bar under the building where Shane lives. We walk several blocks from the subway stop, and as she delivers me to the juice bar, I ask her if it's safe for her to visit Shane like this. She hands me this poem.

Your Kale/Kiwi Juice Has More
Self-Esteem Than I Do

Kale/kiwi juice
just goes in one side
comes out the other
makes everything happier
the whole way through.
It never worries about

being safe or wearing
the right clothes
so no one will treat it
like it doesn't matter.

"This doesn't answer my question," I say. "Are you safe up there by yourself with a guy?"

She tells me they have only ever held hands and kissed. She tells me not to worry, but how can I not worry about China? I have lost track of how many times she has swallowed herself. She just turns herself over and over, esophagus to rectum, like a human Lava Lamp.

She buys me a juice and goes upstairs. I drink the juice and read my book. It's a book about brain-stem function, and though it's interesting, I'm bored by it. I say to myself, *Stanzi, you're in New York City and you're sitting in one place reading a book. You must go outside. It's a lovely day.*

I tell the woman at the juice bar that if my friend comes back, tell her to wait for me. I then ask her if there's anything nice to see in this area and she says we're a block from Central Park, so I walk there and I say to myself, *Stanzi, you're in Central Park. You're in Central Park in New York City.*

I find a bench and I sit down.

I marvel at New York City. But then the questions start.

I ask myself, *Stanzi, why can't you write that poem for English class?*

I ask myself, *Stanzi, why can't you kiss Gustav?*

I ask myself, *Stanzi, what happened to you?*

China Knowles—Monday— Sad Esophagus

A sad esophagus (that's me) and a big-boned girl in a biology lab coat walk into Port Authority at 42nd Street and 8th Avenue in New York City. What happens next is anyone's guess. There are police with bulletproof vests and semiautomatic guns. A lot of them. They are gathered by the doors. Just standing there. People still walk around, going to their buses, their subways, their loved ones.

I watch the police. I look at the guns.

I freeze, just like with the dogs at school.

Stanzi guides me down the corridor where our bus will come pick us up in twenty minutes.

I write Stanzi a note. *Thank you. Sorry again for lying about seeing Gustav's helicopter.*

"It's okay," she says. "Not everyone can see it. No big deal."

"Are you really going to go up in it?" I ask.

"I hope so."

"Aren't you scared?"

"Of what?" she asks.

I take a second to figure out what I'd be most afraid of. "Of it not being real?"

"If it's not real," Stanzi says, "then it's less dangerous than if it *is* real."

"True. But what if it's real? Aren't you afraid to crash?"

"No," she says.

"How can you not be?"

"I have faith. In Gustav. In the helicopter. In ... whatever it is that controls everything."

"God?"

"Whatever."

"Do you know where you'll go?" I ask.

"No. And I don't care. As long as there are no more drills. As long as it makes sense where we're going. Gustav will know."

Our bus arrives and the line moves forward. "Do you love him?" I ask.

Stanzi laughs. "This isn't about love."

"And it's really there? The helicopter?" I ask. "You're the only one who sees it. Lansdale lied. She can't really see it on Fridays."

"I know."

"Do you think his dad sees it?"

"Seems so," I say.

When the bus arrives, Stanzi and I sit next to each other.

She looks out the window, and the bus backs up and pulls out of Port Authority. As we drive toward the tunnel, she looks back at New York City. "So was Shane good? Was seeing him nice?" she asks.

"Yes."

"How old is he?"

"Same. Seventeen."

"Did you meet on Facebook?"

"I don't do that anymore. Not since Irenic Brown," I say, hoping she'll figure it out. Or say something. For once.

"So?" That's all she says.

"I met him on a self-help site."

"Oh."

She doesn't ask what self-help site. She looks out the window after we emerge from the tunnel and she takes in the last view of the city from a distance before the only things to see are marshy NewJerseyscapes and endless highway.

I look at Stanzi and I see that she's crying, so I ask if she's okay.

"Yes."

"Was it something I said?"

"No."

"What, then?"

She turns to me. "Do you love Shane?"

"Yes, I think so," I say.

"That makes me so happy I'm crying."

"Oh. Sorry."

"Don't apologize," she says. "It's a good thing."

86

"I believe, you know. In the helicopter. In the whole thing," I say.

"I'm glad."

"I hope you and Gustav can get out of here. You deserve better."

"So do you."

"You're geniuses."

"So are you," she says.

Stanzi told me once that just because I get bad grades that doesn't make me stupid. She was in my eighth-grade algebra class. She knows the teacher hated me. She knows that's when I started hanging out with my other friends. She told me once that a high percentage of high school dropouts are the smart kids.

I take out my journal and I write in it. Stanzi probably thinks I'm writing about Shane, but I'm really writing about being smart and being stupid at the same time. Getting stoned before a chem final. Drinking gin in the bathroom during ninth-grade study hall. Letting my new friends write my name and number on guys' bathroom stalls.

I never told Shane this, or anyone else, but maybe I deserved what happened to me. Maybe I had it coming since eighth grade. I gave up, so everyone else did, too.

Stanzi—Monday—
Free Shrinks

As the bus nears our station, China says, "I'm sorry if we get in trouble tomorrow."

I shrug to say I don't mind.

"What will you tell your parents?" she asks.

"I'll tell them I got sick of the drills. I'll tell them I'm scared to blow up. I'll tell them that it's finally getting to me."

She nods. "This town needs more shrinks," she says.

"Every town needs more shrinks," I say.

"Free shrinks," she says.

"Yeah," I say.

China says, "That's how I found Shane online. We are all each other's free shrinks. It's a forum for people who have survived things. Maybe you could join."

I can't even figure out how I'd introduce myself to a group of strangers. I don't even know if I need a shrink. Is it normal to know, deep down, that you are two people joined as cells? Is it normal to know, for sure, that there is an organ inside us that no scientist has discovered? Is it normal to know, without a doubt, that you will escape this place in a helicopter that no one else can see? How would I explain that to a roomful of strangers?

"Aren't you going to ask me about why I go online to talk about my problems?" China asks.

I'm still in the imaginary free-shrink room, telling the strangers I wear a lab coat every day. In my imagination, I don't tell them the lab coat keeps me safe, because I'm afraid they'll think I'm crazy.

"I didn't want to make you uncomfortable," I say.

She says, "Look at me." She is a stomach. She is digesting a bag of Swedish Fish she ate on the bus. Everything is red. "Aren't you ever going to ask me what's wrong?" she asks.

"I was waiting until you felt ready," I answer. I don't tell her I can't talk about things like that. I can't tell her anything since the day I lied to her about the scar on my leg. I'd told her it was from a boating accident. She'd said, "That's bullshit and you know it."

Stanzi—Monday—Bears

When I pass the dangerous bush, the man pops out, totally naked. I ask him where his trench coat went and he tells me he's a bear and bears don't wear trench coats. He grabs me with his huge paws and pulls me into the bush. There he has tea set up on an old mahogany table. Proper china cups and all. Gold-leafed rims. Doilies adorn the saucers, the table, under the tiny plates where there are madeleine cookies for us both.

The tea is the perfect temperature.

We toast our good luck. I tell him about my trip to New York City. He tells me his mother lives inside the house and she yells at him all the time even though he's trying to help her be old and die. He tells me he shares letters because he can't stop making them. "I'm an artist," he says.

"They're nice letters," I say. "Very sturdy."

"No one wants them," he says. "No one walks by anymore."

"Most people are scared of you," I explain.

"So why are you here?" he asks.

"It's on the way to Gustav's house and the Mexican restaurant. And I'm not scared of you," I say. "I like your letters."

He gives me a huge wooden *D*. It is painted with tiny dots of every color. I thank him and ask him to keep it for me because it's too big to carry. He asks, "Do you want to go there now?"

"Where?"

"The restaurant?"

I'm hungry. The last thing I ate was the kale/kiwi drink in the juice bar by Central Park. "You have to put some clothes on," I say.

"I know. Wait here. I'll be right back."

I don't wait.

I walk to Gustav's house. I ask him if he'd like to come with me to Las Hermanas. I know he can't resist the tamales.

"I'm starving," Gustav says. "But I don't have any money."

I tell him I'll pay for dinner. I tell him the dangerous bush man is coming with us.

"He's naked," Gustav says. "He's always naked."

"I told him to put clothes on," I say. "He'll be fine. He's a nice man, really. Just bored, I think. Like we're bored, yes? He makes nice letters."

Gustav looks uncomfortable.

"You don't have to come if you don't want to come," I say. "Why are you so uncomfortable about the dangerous bush man? Isn't he helping you with the helicopter? I thought you were friends."

"He makes letters and he gives them to people," Gustav says.

"I know. I have many of his letters," I say.

"You kissed him!" Gustav seems shocked. Or possessive. I can't tell.

"Yes," I say. "A few times. But there are other ways one acquires such quality letters."

He changes the subject.

"There were two bomb threats today," he tells me as he climbs down from the cockpit and puts his tool belt on the bench. "One of them came from New York City," he says. "Nobody knows this but me, but I know you're trying to solve the mystery, so I'm telling you."

I nod but don't ask him about the other bomb threat. It was nice to escape them for a day. I ask him to hurry. "I'm hungry," I say.

When we get outside, the dangerous bush man is there, dressed in a pair of jeans and a T-shirt that says WHAT WOULD YOUR TV DO? The three of us walk to the restaurant and instead of going in and sitting down, Gustav leads us to the takeout window and we order, and though I can see the dangerous bush man is disappointed by this, he knows he is the dangerous bush man as much as I know I'm Stanzi, a character in your book, a nobody and a somebody and really two people inside one body, and as much as Gustav knows he is the boy who is building the invisible helicopter. We are not the three most welcome people in the neighborhood.

Stanzi—Monday Night—
Box Bet Bug Bin

I get a burrito because it's easier to eat while walking and that's what Gustav wants to do—obvious from the fact that he begins his journey home before the bush man and I can leave the restaurant window. Gustav got a Styrofoam container of tamales and the bush man gets *dos pollo* enchiladas and I'm envious because that's what I would have gotten had we gone into the restaurant and sat down like normal people. I do not say this aloud, but the minute I think it, the bush man taps me on the shoulder and gives me his container of enchiladas. I give him my burrito and say thank you. He tells me I'm welcome *en español*. *"De nada."*

When we get to Gustav's garage, Gustav climbs into the invisible cockpit to eat by himself, and the bush man says good-bye and continues on to his house. Or his bush. Or wherever he will eat my burrito.

I sit on the upturned paint bucket and balance the Styro-foam container of enchiladas, rice, and beans on my knees and attempt to eat them with a white plastic knife and fork and Gustav asks, "Why do you even talk to that guy?"

"I feel bad for him."

"He's crazy," Gustav says.

"He gave you the helicopter," I say.

"That doesn't make him sane," Gustav says. "He only gave it to me when I told him I couldn't stand to be alive here anymore."

I don't say anything to this. He must be exaggerating. Maybe it was during his string theory/snowshoe episode last year.

"I don't even know if the thing will fly or not," Gustav says. "He might have given it to me because he wanted me to take my mind off other things."

"Some people would say we're all crazy," I answer. He shoves most of a tamale into his mouth and chews for what feels like an entire minute. I add, "But we're not, of course. I mean, not like that."

Gustav looks at me with a mix of sadness and curiosity in his eyes. "You really have his letters?" he asks. "You really *have* kissed him?"

"Yes."

"Why?"

"Why not?"

"That's not an answer," Gustav says.

"I don't know," I say. "He just wants to be loved. He just wants to give his letters away. They *are* superior letters. I've never seen anything like them."

"Everyone wants to be loved," Gustav says.

We eat the rest of our meal in silence, and when Gustav is finished with his tamales, he picks up his tool belt and goes back to work on his cockpit. I ask him what he's working on and he says he's fastening the control panel now that all of the gauges and switches and dials have been tested. He tells me we'll be ready soon.

"Maybe tomorrow," he says.

"Tomorrow?"

"Tuesday would be the ideal day of the week for us to go," he says.

"I know."

"Do you trust me?" he asks.

"Yes."

"Why?"

"Why not?" I answer.

This time he doesn't press me for more than *Why not?* This time he knows what I mean when I say it. He knows we are not lettered A, B, C, D, or E. He knows we are not mice in a school-shaped plywood maze. He knows I sometimes don't want to be alive here anymore, either.

"You really think...tomorrow?" I ask.

"I think so," he says. "I have to give it a short test in the morning." He looks down at something under his feet—presumably pedals—and says, "After that, we can go."

"I don't understand how we can go to an invisible place," I say. "Is that all the bush man told you?"

"It's a hotbed of genius," he says. "That's what he told me."

"But you told me he said it was invisible."

"He did. But he's also crazy, right?" Gustav answers. "Just imagine a place where you never have to feel like you're in kindergarten again. No assessment, no holding back, and no bullshit."

"Is that what he said it is?"

"I don't know. But that's what I imagined."

I stand there for a minute and try to imagine what *hotbed of genius* looks like to me. I see me curing the world of guilt. I see no more trips with Mama and Pop. "Okay," I say. "My parents must be wondering where I am. I spent the day with China skipping school."

"I wish China could come with us," Gustav says.

"She can't see it," I say.

"Not even on Thursdays?"

"No. She was lying."

"Huh," Gustav says. "She's spending too much time with Lansdale Cruise, maybe. China usually tells the truth."

I don't think anyone usually tells the truth, so I don't say anything.

"What will you bring?" Gustav asks.

I think for a moment and say, "My dissection kit and a lab notebook and my goggles and a change of clothes. Does that sound good?"

"Will you be wearing your lab coat?" he asks, and points to my lab coat.

"Of course," I answer.

"I thought you might leave it here," he says.

"Why?" I ask.

"Why not?" he answers.

I put my empty enchilada container in the trash can in the garage and say, "Good night, Gustav. I'll see you and your lovely red helicopter tomorrow."

He waves and says something about his tachometer.

○○○●○

The man is in his trench coat again. He says, as if he'd never met me before, as if we didn't have bear-tea or trade dinner entrées, "Wanna buy an *A*?"

"I already have an *A*," I say.

He digs around behind the bush. "How about a *C*?"

"Do you have a *W*?"

He roots around again in the bush and comes back with two *V*s. He holds them side by side and they form a child's exaggerated *W*.

"That's two *V*s," I say.

"I know." He pulls his trench coat open and searches the inside pockets. His nakedness is so normal to me by now I don't even notice it. "I have an *M*," he says, and hands it to me. He is joyous about this. He is thrilled that he has an *M*.

"Do you make any numbers?"

"Numbers!" he says. "Ha!"

I turn the letter *M* over in my hands. It is smooth and cold. I ask, "Is this marble?"

"Granite."

"I'll take this *M*," I say. "As a good-bye present."

He squints at me and grins. "Is Gustav finally going?" He is more excited than he was when he found the granite *M* in his trench coat pocket. He holds up his index finger. "Wait," he says, then runs from the bush to the front of his house, and I hear the storm door slam and the sound of someone running up or down a set of wooden stairs.

In a minute, he is standing in front of me again. He says, "I wish I could come with you. I've seen it. It's perfect."

I have no idea what the dangerous bush man is talking about. "What's perfect?"

"They say there are no departures," he says. "But they lie. I've been there. I came back."

"If it's perfect, why did you come back?" I ask.

"Because nothing is perfect," he says. "Perfect is a myth. I want you to remember this. Perfect is a boldfaced lie. It's a ham sandwich without ham. It's a blue sky on Mondays when it rains on Wednesdays."

"Okay," I say, because we could stand here all night talking in crazy bush man circles. "Can I pay you for this quality *M*?"

He looks sad that I've asked. Hurt, even. "It's a gift. You can't take it with you because it's too heavy. But it's a gift all the same."

"Can you see it?" I ask.

"The helicopter?"

"Yes."

"Of course," he says.

"Which day?"

He occupies himself with arranging his letters in order of texture behind the bush. When he leans over too far, his scrotum is just visible through the slit in the back of his trench coat. He stands again. "What do you mean, which day?"

"Which day can you see it?"

"Every day," he says. His face finishes his statement. It says, *Why would you ask such a stupid question?*

"I can only see it on Tuesdays," I say.

He acts as if he doesn't hear me and reaches into his innermost trench coat pocket. He produces what looks like a map. It looks very used. It looks old. Yellowed. He says, "There is only one of these. Gustav will know what to do with it." He grabs my shoulders and says, "This is *the only one.* Do you understand?"

I take the map and tuck it under the elbow that is braced against my side because it's still holding the granite *M.* I feel dejected because we're not kissing. It makes no sense. No one should want the dangerous bush man to kiss them.

I open the map and look at it by the light of the streetlamp. I can't understand the markings or the drawings, really. All I can see are two lines of text. At the top it reads THE PLACE OF ARRIVALS. At the bottom it reads THERE ARE NO DEPARTURES.

I wonder if this is all a joke.

The dangerous bush man says, "Do I look like I'm joking?"

I wonder if I was talking my thoughts aloud.

He says, "No. I can hear them."

I think about how I want him to kiss me.

He grabs me by the shoulders and kisses me softly on the forehead. "You go sleep," he says. "It's a long journey."

I nod.

"Don't show anyone the map except Gustav. Not even when you get there," he says. "*Especially* when you get there."

I walk home.

When I get to the front door, I put the *M* and the map in my backpack. I check my phone and see it's nearly eleven o'clock and I guess Mama and Pop will be waiting up to ask me where I was all day.

But there is only a note.

Gone to bed. TV dinner in freezer. Make sure you turn out the lights.

I don't know why they leave that note about going to bed. I checked a long time ago. They're not in bed. They're in another three-letter-word-that-starts-with-a-*B*. They are in a box. They are in a bet. A but. A bug. A bin. They are in a bog. They are in a boy. A bit. A ban. A bap.

Or they are in a bar.

More specifically, they're at Chick's Bar, which is just down the street from our house. Two hundred and twelve steps, to be exact. Architects built the community this way. With bars. And playgrounds. They're near each other so parents can watch their kids fall off the swing set from their barstool and then try to sober up on the way to the hospital for clavicle X-rays.

Patricia—Monday—Standstill

IN THE PLACE OF ARRIVALS

I hear music all the time. Since I can remember.

All sorts of music.

Sometimes other people's music. Sometimes my music.

Sometimes my music has helicopters in it.

The *thwap-thwap-thwap, thwap-thwap-thwap, thwap-thwap-thwap*.

I'm forty-three years old and I've written 167 symphonies, 598 pop songs, 134 jazz numbers, fifty-six rock-and-roll/punk rock/heavy metal riffs. I can mix records on three turntables at a time and I'm the only creator, as far as I know, of a scratch-dub-trap-hip-hop opera. I've written twelve of them.

But I haven't written anything in a year. I'm at a standstill. I hear partial music—bits of songs in my head, but I don't hear what I used to. There are instruments missing.

I miss Kenneth since he left us. I miss Kenneth because

there weren't supposed to be any departures. Once you come here, you stay here. That's the deal. Kenneth broke the rules and left. In doing so, he reminded me why I wrote twelve scratch-dub-trap-hip-hop operas.

The whole idea is to break the rules. The whole idea is to break the fucking rules. So I stopped. Time stopped. Everything is focused on departure.

And today I hear a song. Today's song has helicopters.

This can mean only one thing.

Arrivals.

Stanzi—Tuesday Morning— The Trained Escapist

"The principal called us yesterday!"

This is my alarm clock on my last day. It's Mama and she's saying things too quickly. It is 5:34 a.m. Mama has been watching morning news since five.

"She said you skipped school. She said you were in trouble. Maybe that you sent these bomb threats," she says.

I sit up and wipe the sleep from my eyes. It's still not late enough to be light. She's standing in my doorway and is about to switch on my light and I say, "Please don't turn on the light," but she turns it on anyway.

"Did you?"

"Of course not," I answer. "I know who's sending the bomb threats, I think. I'm still investigating."

"I mean skipping school," she says.

"Oh."

"Did you?"

"Yes."

"Where did you go?"

"With China. To see her boyfriend," I say.

Mama looks suddenly happy. "She has a boyfriend? That's nice," she says. "Good for her."

"Can you go now?"

"Who do you think is sending the bomb threats?" she asks.

"I can't tell you until I know for sure," I say.

"Where does China's boyfriend live?"

"Philadelphia," I lie.

"Did you drink alcohol?"

"No."

"Did you smoke marijuana?"

"Of course not."

"Did he have guns in his house?" she asks.

"I didn't ask. I wasn't really in his house. I was at some kind of restaurant."

She thinks for a minute. "You let her go to a boy's house alone?"

"Yes. She made me."

"She's going to end up in the looney tunes with that other friend of yours, I swear it."

"She's saner than you'd think," I say. *She's saner than you*, I think.

"There was a shooting last night in a movie theater in Florida," she says.

"That's nice," I say.

"What did you eat in the restaurant in Philadelphia?"

"Kale/kiwi juice smoothie thing. It was nice."

Mama makes a face. This is finally what pries her from my doorway and back to her television. Green food.

I put my blankets over my face to block the light and realize this could be the last day I see Mama. *There are no departures.* I expected to feel some deep pull, as if there is a maternal elastic band attached to my stomach; I feel nothing but sadness for her.

You can see it in our family picture albums—her decline. Her face fell. Her eyes went dark. The morbid outings started. The master list was made. The peanut butter and jelly crackers, the picnic blankets. The emergency plans for everything imaginable. Fire, intruder, explosion, gas leak, sinkhole. I'm a trained escapist.

Today will be easy for me.

I have been practicing for as long as I can remember.

When I finally get up, I remove the granite *M* from my backpack and put it on my desk. I pack (no schoolbooks, all clothing and other things I want to take with me) and take a shower. I hear them talking in the kitchen on my way from the bathroom back to my room.

Pop says, "Maybe we should call the counselor again."

Mama says, "He always said it would catch up with her."

Pop says, "I wish she'd take off that damn coat."

Mama says, "I think it's getting bad now. She lied to me. She never lied before."

Pop says, "I can make an appointment for tomorrow, I bet. He always saw us last minute when she was little."

Mama sighs. "God."

Pop says, "She's alive, Mama. It's a blessing. We just need to help her."

Mama says, "I can't help. I don't want to think about it."

Pop says, "I don't, either. But it's the only way we can help her."

Mama says, "You take her."

Pop says, "I'll get an appointment for as soon as we can."

Mama says, "She needs help."

Pop says, "He'll talk to her. He remembers us. He'll help."

Mama says, "I think she's the bomb threat. I think she's the one."

I close my door then—loudly enough for them to hear. Mama is wrong about the bomb threat. We are all the bomb threat.

The doorbell sounds and I know it's China because she told me we'd walk to school together today.

I'm not even close to ready.

Ready for school, or ready to tell her I'm not coming to school, or ready to tell her I'm going away with Gustav today.

I tell Mama to let her in and I get dressed and let my hair dry itself. It gets curly when I let it dry naturally. As I get ready, China looks at my new letter *M*. She doesn't ask me about it.

I heave my backpack onto my back and China asks, "What's in that thing?"

I tell her it's my books, even though she knows my books are still in my locker from before we skipped yesterday. I reach into my lab coat pocket and retrieve the poem.

"I finished my poem. For English," I say.

She reads it to herself.

Reset. Reset. Reset.

There is a tiny hole
and if you unbend a paper clip
and insert it into the hole,
the world resets.
It becomes a giant liver
three lobes
wrapped around a heart.
It filters.
It regenerates.
We grow grass on it
eat our picnics on the grass
we make love on it
never knowing
that we are the filter.

"It's good for a first poem," China says.

"Thanks."

"I hope she gives you an A," she says.

"She can give me any letter she wants," I say.

When we walk out of my room, Mama and Pop are still

sitting at the kitchen table, half glued to the TV morning shows and half talking about how they're going to make an appointment for me. I see Pop attempt to get my attention, but I ignore him.

I don't say good-bye. Not even to my cat.

When I close the door, something shivers in me as if I know I'm colder now.

Patricia—Tuesday Morning—
Thwap-thwap-thwap

IN THE PLACE OF ARRIVALS

I tell Gary that there will be arrivals and he tells me I need to
get more sleep.

"But there *will* be arrivals," I say. "I hear them."

I realize telling Gary is probably not a good idea, so I pretend it was a dream. I sit up and shake my head. I say, "Did I
just say something?"

Gary says, "I don't think so."

"I just had the weirdest dream," I say. "What time is it?"

"Seven."

"Huh," I say. Then I go into the kitchen to make myself
tea while Gary goes to the bathroom. He's loud when he shits.
It's one of the many things I hate about him.

There is no marriage here. Just housing arrangements.
Cooking schedules. Roommates with benefits. Gary isn't even
my friend. I'm a convenience and he's a philosopher who's

convinced that the real world was only made for dumb people. He hasn't realized yet that he's dumb, too.

I sit at the kitchen table and send a message to the arrivals. I say, *Turn back! This is a prison!* But I think of the possibility of departure and realize it could be my turn.

Gary never knew about Kenneth and me. To Gary, Kenneth was just the nudist—an artist incapable of social interaction on Gary's level. The nudist lived in his own hut, by himself. He didn't like visitors. That's all Gary knew.

The flush sounds and Gary is in the kitchen.

"Coming to breakfast today?" he asks.

I hold my head. "This migraine is coming on again. I think I might skip it."

"Want me to bring you something back?"

"Sure. Whatever," I say. "I'm going to lie down for a while."

When he leaves, I pull out the last thing Kenneth ever gave me. A small carved letter *P*. He carved it from a piece of quartz we found on a walk one day. I must have been twenty-five then.

I can't believe I've been here this long. The only reason I stayed was Kenneth. I wrote him many symphonies and he carved me letters and left them in places where I'd see them.

The letters are still where he left them—throughout the forest, even in the dining hall and the meeting rooms—but none of the others see them. I know this means something, but I don't know what.

I know this means I don't belong here, but I can't figure out how to leave.

China Knowles—Tuesday Morning—Gallbladder

I am China—the gallbladder, walking to school.

Stanzi is being weird. Beyond lab-coat weird.

As we walk, she wants to take *that* road. The one with the bush.

I tell her she knows I don't ever walk down that road. She tells me it's an easier way to Gustav's house and she has to go that way.

"Anyway," she says, "the man in the bush works during the day."

I get angry too quickly about this statement. She pretends I haven't seen the letters in her room. Like I don't know how she got them. I feel like Stanzi isn't my friend at all. What real friend would ignore all these signs I give her? What real friend wouldn't ask about Irenic Brown and what happened, after reading all my poems about it? What real friend would make me walk down *that* road knowing all my secrets?

How to Know If Your Dangerous Bush Man Is Real

If the man hiding in the dark bush
gives you a letter
when you kiss him
then he is probably real.
If the man hiding in the dark bush
frightens you
when you just glimpse
the road
then he is most likely real.
When the man hiding in the dark bush
has become a friend
of your friend
and she defends him
as if he is normal
as if he is a simple character in the neighborhood
as if his kisses
are worth it
then he is certainly real.
When the man hiding in the dark bush
makes you wonder
if you couldn't be more forgiving
then there is no doubt he is real.
Every town has shadows
where we hide mythical
beasts.
Mythical beasts.

I walk down the road with Stanzi, and I hear a strange sound. A muffled *thwap-thwap-thwap*.

Stanzi says, "Do you hear that?"

I say yes, I hear that.

I look at her and see what she's always told me about. There are two of her. Clearly. She is split down the middle. Sliced in two. When I look, I see that one of her eyes is blue and one is brown. When I look harder, I see that one of her hands is trying to make the other hand wave good-bye to me. Half of her mouth wants to tell me the truth while the other half must lie.

I ask her why the helicopter is so quiet.

"Maybe because it's invisible?" she answers.

As we get to Gustav's backyard, I can tell she sees it. Her eyes light up. Gustav is standing on the grass, lifting a box above his head and shoving it inside. I can't see the helicopter. I can still hear a faint *thwap-thwap-thwap*.

I ask Stanzi if today is the day she's leaving us.

"Yes."

I hug her and stand by myself on the sidewalk as she goes to Gustav.

My gallbladder cries because it is the only part anyone can see and it is the place where my tears decide to come out and it's at this moment I know I must reappear.

I must come back.

If Stanzi isn't here to protect me and Gustav is taking his genius elsewhere, I will be alone in a sea of number two pencils.

Right there on the sidewalk outside Gustav's house, I turn myself right side in. I shake my hair into place. I take a deep breath and approach Stanzi, who is now helping Gustav load the helicopter.

"Who will read my poetry now that you're gone?"

She says, "You'll have to read it yourself."

"Do you have an address?"

She looks at me and shrugs.

When Gustav goes inside to get more stuff, I ask, "Are you sure this is safe? Are you sure you want to do this?"

"I'm sure."

"Has he ever flown a helicopter before?" I ask.

"Does it matter?" she answers.

I'm Stanzi's friend and I know her secrets. A person doesn't go through what Stanzi went through and turn out just fine except for the lab coat. I'm being a bad friend. I should call her parents now. Tell them everything that's happening.

A man's voice comes from behind me. "And who would believe your story about an invisible helicopter?"

When I turn and see the man in his trench coat, I sprint toward school.

○○○○●

When I get to school, I find Lansdale and she is shocked that I have become a girl again and not a digestive system on legs. She says, "I'm proud of you."

And I'm proud of myself, too.

Two boys walk by and say, "Nice to see you again, China."

A teacher gives me a sympathetic look as if he knows—as if he saw what everyone else saw on Facebook, and I'm suddenly like one of those popping toys you can get in a quarter machine at the supermarket—the kind you press concave until they slowly right themselves and pop up high into the air.

Lansdale Cruise looks on in horror as my insides swallow my outsides again, instantly. She looks a mix of disappointed and disgusted.

"Bummer."

"Yeah," I say, with a mouth full of myself.

"I guess some things can't be helped."

"I can be helped."

"We'll keep working on it," Lansdale says.

Stanzi—Tuesday Morning—
Splitting in Two

After I watch China run away, I think: *It's hard to trust your helicopter pilot.*

I can feel a laugh and a scream forming at the same time. I'm frozen, standing here with my backpack at my feet, looking up at the beauty of his red helicopter.

I distract myself with questions. *How long did it take him? When did he start? He said he'd get credit in AP physics for this. He hasn't mentioned that since, though. I wonder why.*

Teachers don't give credit for something they can't see.

"Who needs credit?" the dangerous bush man says. "You're going to a place of no credit."

I look at him and say, "Aren't you supposed to be at work?"

"Took the day off," he says. "Wanted to make sure you two got out of here okay."

"Why wouldn't we?"

He looks at me. I think he can see me splitting in two. "Are you okay?" he asks.

"Of course."

He studies me. "One part of you wants to stay and one part of you wants to go. Is that correct?"

I nod.

"This is normal."

I nod again.

"He'll be a good pilot. I taught him everything I know."

I think about kissing Gustav the way I have kissed the dangerous bush man.

He says, "I recommend this."

I try not to think anything else important while he's there. Mind readers make me uncomfortable. I have too many thoughts.

"You shouldn't be afraid," he says. "Once you get there, find Patricia and tell her I miss her." He walks over to Gustav and says something to him about how I have the map and he helps him lift a box into the helicopter and he slips a small, blocky, glittery letter *P* from his coat pocket and puts it inside the box without Gustav seeing.

Inside my head, I hear his voice. *Give that letter to her. She'll know I sent you. She'll take care of you. You can trust her. She's a very good friend.*

○○○●○

Gustav and I climb into the helicopter. It's not like the opening credits to *M*A*S*H* where the dust and trees act frenzied

117

by the wind. It's calm. The sound is no louder than a purring cat, and I can feel the subtle movement of the rotor and the turbine that will fly us to wherever Patricia is. I've latched on to her in under a minute. She will be our camp counselor. Our friend. That's what the bush man said. *She's a very good friend.*

Gustav turns to me and says, "Are you ready?"

I nod.

"You have to say yes or no. I don't want anyone thinking I kidnapped you."

"What a strange thing to say," I say.

"I need you to say loud and clear that you want to do this," he says.

"I want to do this. But I want you to kiss me first."

Gustav recoils. "I'm afraid to kiss."

"I'll teach you."

He seems willing, so before I strap myself into the passenger's seat, I lean over to him and I kiss him gently on the lips over and over until he begins to kiss me back and we do this for several minutes.

He straps himself into the pilot's seat. He checks his gauges. He puts on his headset and I put mine on and he checks communication between us by saying, "That was a very nice kiss."

I check my communication device by answering, "I've loved you for two years, only I couldn't tell you."

He doesn't answer this because he's busy flipping switches and firing up the helicopter to full speed and he asks, "Are you ready?"

"Yes."

I look out onto the lawn where I was standing only five minutes before and I see her—my other Stanzi. She is staying here, in the land of test drills, bomb drills, and mourning parents, and I will finally escape. I wave to her. I don't know why she's smiling.

I'm the one who should be smiling.

I'm the one who is escaping.

Patricia—Tuesday Morning—
We Are Rotting

IN THE PLACE OF ARRIVALS

Gary brings me a hard-boiled egg.

He says, "What are you doing today?"

I say, "I don't know. Probably working in the garden."

He disapproves. I know this because he disapproves every day.

"You don't really have a migraine, do you?" he asks.

"The rest helped," I lie.

Even though lying isn't allowed, we all do it.

Even though conforming isn't allowed, asking us all not to lie is conforming.

It's no different, even though it was supposed to be different.

None of us are leaders.

None are followers.

Essentially, we are rotting.

"Why aren't you composing?" Gary asks.

"I don't know."

"Still sore about what I said last time I asked?" he says.

Gary and I fight over this all the time. I tell him my music is nothing without listeners. He tells me I'm being greedy because I only want to make money from the music's listeners. I say something like "Is that so bad?" and then he shakes his head as if I'm some leech on the world.

What good is it doing here?

He says the joy is the creation.

He says sharing it will sully it.

I say sharing is the whole point.

He calls me a child—because he's fifty-two and I'm forty-three. He calls me a child for wanting to share talent. Isn't that what you do with talent?

Isn't that what you do?

Stanzi—Wednesday—Coffins

I miss her. My other. She's down there while I'm up here. She has my hands, my lips, and my nose. I have everything else. Neither of us can see Gustav's helicopter on a Wednesday.

I slept last night. Gustav doesn't even grow sleepy. He says he's wide awake. He says, "No drills today for us."

I think of my parents and I miss them. I think of the week's worth of freezer food that they bought for me to heat up, and wonder if they will eat it now that I'm gone.

Or will she go and take my place? Can she?

I move my hands and purse my lips. I wiggle my nose.

I don't know what I left back in Gustav's yard, but it wasn't her. She's here with me. But part of me is gone.

I say, "Is it dumb for me to miss home?"

Gustav says, "Depends what you call home."

I say, "I miss China. I even miss Lansdale and her lies."

"You only left yesterday," he says.

"China needs me," I say.

Quiet grows between us.

"What happened to China?" he asks. "Why did she swallow herself?"

"I think it has something to do with a boy," I say.

"Irenic Brown," Gustav says.

"Yeah," I say.

"Look. It isn't really a secret, is it? Not with pictures for everyone to see," he says.

I didn't look at them. I knew they were there. I heard, but my ears didn't want to listen. I try to pretend things are normal, the way Mama and Pop pretend they go to bed early every night.

I tell Gustav, "I have dreams about coffins. And sometimes Adolf Hitler."

He nods. "Why Adolf Hitler?"

"Why not?" I answer. "I have dreams about cheese, too. Can't choose what you dream about."

"True," he says.

I say, "In one of them, Adolf Hitler is a huge beetle and he eats all the other beetles. Even his own kind. And there's another one where everyone at school knows how to waltz but we don't know how to waltz."

"I'm pretty sure Adolf Hitler knew how to waltz," Gustav says.

"I mean you and me. We don't know how to waltz," I say.

"Oh," he says. "I'm in your dreams?"

"All the time."

"With the coffins?"

"Yes."

"Are we dead?"

"Yes. But then no. It depends which dream. You're always in the red coffin."

"Does Hitler have a coffin?" he asks.

"Yes. It's black," I say.

"Seems right," Gustav says. He asks, "Does anyone dance with him?"

"No. I don't think so. He's always the bug eating other bugs. But one time he had lederhosen on and was exercising his hamstrings."

"Are there drills in your dreams?" he asks.

"Sometimes there are bombs, too. And the dangerous bush man," I say.

"He's a good neighbor," Gustav says.

"He is."

"And you've kissed him for letters," Gustav says. "But you've never kissed me until yesterday."

I think about this before I answer. "I didn't think you wanted me to kiss you," I say.

"I've been busy," Gustav says.

I want to touch a part of the helicopter to emphasize that I know he's been busy—to tell him how genius he was to build it—but it's not there. Not the body, not the windscreen, not even the seat I'm sitting in. If I think about it for too long, I grow frightened, so I focus on the hem of my lab coat. I fiddle

124

with the fat corner where all the fabric meets. I slip my thumb-
nail into the tiny groove left by the sewing machine.

"Do you have any other dreams?" Gustav asks. "Dreams
without coffins?"

"Yes," I say.

"Do you want to tell me about them?" he asks.

"No," I say.

"Am I in them?" he asks.

"Mozart is in them," I say. "And I'm Stanzi. And we're
happy. And everything is falling apart."

"Mozart doesn't get a coffin, does he?" Gustav asks.

I do not explain that the movie *Amadeus* is fictitious. I
let Gustav believe that genius is often disregarded. That's the
point of the film, and I allow Gustav his fictions.

"Why did the dangerous bush man have the map?" I ask.

"Clearly, he's been here before," Gustav answers.

"I think he's harmless," I say. "I don't think he really puts
roofies in the lemonade he sells. I think it's a joke to him."

"He's a very funny man," Gustav says.

"I never knew this about him," I answer.

The Interviews—
Wednesday

Interview #1 Lansdale Cruise

The man arrives at Lansdale Cruise's house. The Cruises are undergoing construction. They are cutting Mrs. Cruise #4 out of their lives as if she'd never been there. The white couches are being loaded into a truck. The glass-topped dining table. The impossible stair-climbing machine that never got her anywhere. Just always climbing.

"Do you know where the missing kids could be?" the man asks Lansdale Cruise.

She plays with her hair. "They're on a boat," she says. "With many fishing rods." She smiles. "Just kidding. They're on a hunting trip with a rifle."

"They're armed?"

"No," she says. "I was kidding about that, too."

"Where are they?"

"I don't know."

"We think you know more than you say you do."

"Doesn't everyone?" she asks. "I have the answers," she says.

"And?"

"I have them memorized in sentences."

"And?"

"And bats eat cold dogs after being coy animals during deadly Easter attacks due at any basic daily cat appreciation dance."

He looks at her, frustrated.

"Those are the answers," she says. "Just the first twenty-one of them. Do you want more?"

He turns to his cameraman. "Cut it."

"What's wrong?" she asks. "Were those not the right answers?"

"We'll ask your friends. Someone has to know what happened."

"But the answers were right!" Lansdale argues. "I know it! ABECDABCADDEADAABDCAD. That's the sequence!"

"Mr. Cruise? Can we ask you a few questions?"

Mr. Cruise is directing the moving men to take a painting off the wall. It's not a real painting. It is glitter and shiny fabric glued to a canvas. He doesn't answer.

The man asks again. "It's about the two missing kids."

Mr. Cruise answers, "What do I know about kids? Does it look like I know anything about kids?"

Lansdale says, "He's right. He's never here. He never met them."

"Weren't they your friends?" the man asks.

Lansdale looks sad. "Yes."

"Do you know they were the ones sending the bomb threats?"

"No, they weren't."

"How do you know?"

"Because I know who was sending the bomb threats."

"And?"

"And it wasn't them," Lansdale says. "Now go away."

The man walks with his cameraman out of the driveway and down the sidewalk. He says, "I swear her hair grew while I was talking to her. Did you see that?"

The cameraman answers, "You weren't looking at her hair."

The man says, "I know, right?"

Lansdale hears this and says, "They send two morons like you to ask questions? You don't even know the answers when you hear them!"

Interview #2 Gustav's father

"They left in the helicopter on Tuesday morning," he says.

"Who did?"

"My boy and his friend. The girl in the white coat."

"Where's the helicopter?"

"It was in my garage. Now it's somewhere else."

"Why do you seem unworried by this?"

"Because Gustav knows what he's doing," he says. "The boy is smarter than all of us put together. He has an IQ of a hundred and seventy-six."

"The police say there wasn't any helicopter," the man says.

"The police don't *believe*."

The man chuckles. "So, you have to *believe* to see the helicopter?"

"Yes."

"And did you see them take off?"

"I was at work yesterday morning. I start at seven."

"So you don't really know, then. Is that what you're saying?"

"The helicopter was here. Now it isn't. And my boy is gone with the girl who sat here and watched him build it. Anyone with a brain can figure that out. Don't know why you're all making a big deal. They're big kids. Smart kids. They'll be fine."

"He built the helicopter?"

"Yes."

"He built a helicopter that no one could see?"

"I could see it."

"Can you show me any proof of it?"

Gustav's father points to his empty garage. "There's your proof right there. Do you see a helicopter?"

"No."

"Well."

"But no one could see it before yesterday, either," the man says.

Gustav's father says, "Why don't you have a real job instead of this? I bet your hands are as soft as breasts."

"Interesting comparison," the man says.

"Nothing is softer than breasts," Gustav's father says.

Interview #3 Irenic Brown's parents

"We don't know anything about it," they say, in unison. They are one voice. They are two-people-in-one. They are an *it*. They repeat themselves. "We don't know anything about it."

"We understand your boy goes to school with them."

"Does he?"

"He dated her best friend, didn't he? That's what we hear."

"Whose best friend?"

"The missing girl. She wore a lab coat. Her name is _____."

It looks at each other. It says, "He dates a lot of girls."

The man and the cameraman look at each other and shrug.

"Your son has an unusual name," the man says.

"We named him the day we picked him up," it says. "He was our peace. That's what it means, you know."

"Yes. I know."

"What does that have to do with anything? Why are you here?" it asks.

"We're just interviewing kids who knew them. We're trying to find the truth."

It looks perplexed and defensive. It's a perplexed and defensive machine.

"So Irenic was adopted?" the man asks.

"Not like it's any of your business," it says.

"As a baby?"

"Not like it's any of your business," it says again.

"We heard that he has a reputation," the man says.

"He does. We're very proud."

The man frowns. "I'm not sure you know the exact reputation we're talking about."

"Don't believe rumors you hear," it says. "Our boy wouldn't hurt a living thing. Not even a fly."

"He doesn't hurt flies?" the man asks.

"Not any living thing," it says.

"So the rumors aren't true?"

"I don't know what you're talking about," it says.

"The rumors. About the girls."

"I don't know what you're talking about," it says.

Interview #4 Stanzi's parents

Stanzi's parents have left a note on the kitchen table. It says *Gone to bed. TV dinner in freezer. Make sure you turn out the lights.*

Interview #5 China Knowles

China is a glowing red tongue today. When the man approaches, she waves and accidentally licks his arm.

He asks a series of questions, but China hands him a poem.

You Shouldn't Worry About Gustav and Stanzi

If we were made of paper
then rain could disintegrate us.
So they are safe.

The man reads the poem and he shows it to the cameraman. They look at China-the-tongue. They do not see from her tongue how well she's been eating. They can't see the spinach/apple juice she drank for breakfast. They look away.

The man asks, "Did you see the helicopter?"

China doesn't answer.

"Do you know anything about where they went?"

China writes a haiku.

They went wherever
They had to go to escape
All the tests and drills

"The bomb threats? Is that right? Is that what you mean?" the man asks.

China writes another haiku.

You think we're stupid
You cannot divide fractions
Or dissect a frog

The cameraman reads the haiku and says, "I can divide fractions."

The man says, "I always hated math."

China hands them another poem and then walks into her house.

How to Know If Your Dangerous Bush Man Is Real II

If he is naked
adorned with letters

if his trench coat
is open
then your dangerous bush man
is probably real.
If he holds the answers
and everyone
avoids the street where
he lives
even though they
want the answers
then your dangerous bush man
is most likely real.
If you find a burrito wrapper
disintegrating under a bush
and a sign for lemonade
and a jar full of
tears—a contained ocean—
then you should stop
and ask your dangerous bush man
if he is okay.

The man tries to ask one of China's little sisters if she knows where Gustav and Stanzi are. China's mother comes out, dressed in a neck-to-ankle black latex bodysuit, and says, "Fuck off!"

Interview #6 The school principal
"Do you have any idea how little time I have for this?" she asks.

"We won't take much time," the man says, handing her a release form.

She signs it and sighs. "All I know is that _____ skipped school on Monday with China Knowles. China was in school today. I don't know where the others are. The police are looking into it."

"Where do you think they went?"

"How would I know?"

"Someone told us they left because of the bomb threats," the man says. "Can you tell us more about these threats?"

"No."

"Can you confirm that there have been bomb threats?"

"Can't you read a paper? Or use the Internet?"

The man smiles. "Well, I know and you know that there are bomb threats. But our viewers don't know," he says. "We're national. This is . . . just a little town."

"You'll have to talk to the police. They're handling it now."

"Did you get a bomb threat today?" the man asks. "I see all your students standing outside."

"It's testing week. We give them a break sometimes."

The cameraman steps up on a chair and films the hole in her floor—just to the right of her chair. It's how she gets to work every day. Through the hole. Climbs in. Climbs out.

She looks at them. "Can't you see I'm busy?"

The camera pans wide and shows the principal inside an impossible stack of paperwork from every side. The paperwork is twenty feet high. It's twenty feet wide. It's a great white shark and she is its victim, her torso and arms and head the only things left showing.

Interview #7 The local police chief

"Aren't you the guy on Channel Twelve with the stupid weatherman? What's his name?" the police chief asks.

"I'm national."

"But I saw you. You're on Channel Twelve, right?"

"If Channel Twelve is a CBS affiliate, then yes, maybe that's me. But I'm national."

"You're national? What the hell is that supposed to mean?"

The man stands straight. "It means I flew here from LA last night so I could cover this story."

"What story's that?"

"The disappearance of two teenagers."

"And?" the police chief answers. "Kids disappear every damn day, don't they, Mr. National?"

"Not usually in invisible helicopters, they don't," the man says.

"That's your story?" the police chief says. He laughs. It's unstoppable laughter. It shakes the whole town like an earthquake.

Interview #8 The bartender at the Hilton

The man orders a double. The cameraman orders a lemon-lime soda. The cameraman doesn't usually go to bars.

The wineglasses hanging upside down above the bar

counter are clinking into each other and making a noise that has emptied the bar. The hanging light fixtures are swinging.

"Do you get many earthquakes out this way?" the man asks.

The bartender, who is sweeping up broken glasses as each one falls onto the floor of the back bar, says, "Never."

The man drinks his double quickly. "I'm from LA. We get them there."

"Do they ever stop?" the bartender asks.

"Of course." The man sucks on an ice cube and spits it back into the glass. "Do you know anything about the two kids who disappeared on Tuesday?"

The bartender is kneeling on the back bar floor with a dustpan and brush as more and more glasses shake their way off the bar's shelves. "How the hell should I know?"

The man orders another double to take back to his room. The cameraman slots five quarters into a vending machine and buys a bottle of water. As they head for the elevator, they see the door is stuck open and the alarm light is flashing.

The line for checkout at the Hilton is inexplicably long.

Patricia—Wednesday—
Chewing Gum

IN THE PLACE OF ARRIVALS

Gary tells me I'm playing at breakfast today.

"Playing what?" I ask.

"Anything you want," he answers.

"The piano in the dining hall isn't tuned."

"No one cares. We just want to hear you play," he says. "You used to play for us all the time. Meals aren't the same without it."

I've heard them say this before. Each one, in turn, as if they are primary-school children practicing for a play. They may know how to do many things, but acting isn't one of them.

It won't stop—the *thwap-thwap-thwap*.

I dreamed last night that it's Kenneth coming to rescue me. I miss the most mediocre things. Junk food. Movies. I miss chewing gum, even though I never chewed it much back in the real world. I miss people—any people. I miss walking during rush hour in a big city.

"Why don't you play something classical?" Gary asks.

I get out of bed and get dressed in the same clothing I wore yesterday. There is still garden dirt on the knees. I don't think I should play classical. If Gary had asked me to play punk rock, I wouldn't want to play that, either.

At breakfast, we sit around our usual tables and eat whatever we have. I eat two hard-boiled eggs and a handful of strawberries. Gary tells me I should eat toast because the bread is going stale. I say, "Let it go stale."

I think: *Everything is stale.*

I sit at the piano before the others are finished eating. They pretend not to notice, but I see them smiling at one another. Until I play a half-baked dubstep track that's been running through my head—that's when they stop smiling. It's old. Probably from the 1990s. I wrote it before dubstep had a name. It has lyrics, but I don't sing them because they don't allow swearing here. When I finish and look up at their faces, it's the same look I used to get in high school—a mix of disappointment and sheer confusion.

Whatever.

They clap when I stand up, and I give an animated bow, grab a third hard-boiled egg, and go back to the house.

Gary says, skipping to keep up with me, "Seems silly to waste time on this hip-hop rubbish when you're capable of the classics."

"What are the classics?" I ask. "Do you want me to write

a Gregorian chant because your college professor in the one music class you took in 1979 told you it's relevant?"

"You're not yourself," he says.

I'm not myself. I am a ham sandwich without the ham. I am a blue sky on a Monday and a rainy Wednesday.

I didn't think I loved Kenneth when he was here. Now I think about him all the time. Cliché isn't supposed to exist here, but it does. I didn't know what I had until it was gone. I threw the baby out with the bathwater. Absence makes the heart grow fonder. I've been looking at the world through rose-tinted glasses.

It's not so great, you know.

There is no such thing as individuality when one is part of a collective of people who think they're all individuals. It's a little like being part of a motorcycle club. The idea was to take off on my own and be free. Instead, I'm barreling down an imaginary road alongside a bunch of loud, unruly children.

Stanzi—Thursday Morning—Doomed

We're doomed. I haven't told Gustav this yet because he wouldn't understand. Being doomed isn't like building an invisible helicopter. Being doomed isn't like watching *Amadeus* for the fiftieth time.

Being doomed is being a passenger in a helicopter I can't see for two whole days.

It's like gliding, but while sitting down.

Being doomed asks questions.

Why haven't we run out of fuel yet?

Where are we going?

Why does this map take us in so many circles?

As if Gustav senses my nervousness, he frowns. "Is everything okay?" he asks.

"No," I say. "We're doomed."

"Doomed?" Gustav says.

"Why haven't we stopped for gas?" I say. "And why haven't we stopped at all? We've been up here for two days."

"You need a snack," Gustav says. "You need water."

I look behind me at the box of food Gustav brought. He favors chewy granola bars, raisins, and gum.

"Gum?" I say. "Why did you bring gum?"

Gustav laughs. He points. "We'll land there," he says.

Below us is a green landscape. Flat. No airport. No fuel trucks. Just a field. Gustav is a very good pilot. He lands us smoother than when Mama sits down on a hemorrhoid.

China Knowles—
Thursday—Runaways
Always Come Back

I am China-who-swallowed-herself. I'm China-the-walking-throat. I'm China-being-digested. I'm looking at my mother in her black latex bodysuit. She's forty-two and her body could pass for twenty-five. Dad's coming home. There's a party tonight. There will be strangers in my basement begging for mercy.

I miss Stanzi and Gustav.

I'm sick of Lansdale Cruise because she can't be trusted. Yesterday she told me during the drill that she has leukemia. In a week she will tell me it's in remission. She has done this two times before. The whole cycle makes me feel like a basketball being dribbled.

We walked to school together today and I told her I missed Stanzi and Gustav, but she said they'd be back.

"Runaways always come back," she said.

But we both know that's not true.

I ask Mom, "Is it true that runaways always come back?"

"I don't know," she says. "Some do. Some don't."

"Okay."

"Is there something I should know?" she asks.

"I don't know," I answer. "Maybe later."

I go to Stanzi's house to see her parents. They look worried and ask me if I think Stanzi is okay.

"Gustav is a very trustworthy boy," I say. "They'll be back. I know it." Right then, my esophagus clenches and I feel like I might vomit, so I walk out the front door and go home.

I call Shane and he tells me he ran away lots of times and never went back. He says, "What makes you so sure that Stanzi and Gustav will come home?"

I say, "Because Stanzi knows I need her."

"Life isn't all about you," Shane says.

"That's not fair."

"Nothing's fair," he says.

"I want to run away, too," I say.

"So do it."

"Are you home tomorrow?"

"Yes."

"I'll come to you, then. Around noon."

He sounds happy. "I'll see you then."

But by the time I say *I love you*, he hangs up and my esophagus morphs into stomach walls, coated in acid.

When I get back home, four cars are parked in the driveway. The door isn't locked. I go to my bedroom and pack a bag for running away.

How to Know If Your Runaway Plan Is Real

If you've given up on
every
possible
solution
to an unmentionable problem,
then your plan to run away is probably real.
If you've packed three bags of trail mix,
a curling iron you won't ever use,
three quality letters that spell C-A-N,
then your plan to run away is most likely real.
If you don't cry
and you feel nearly human
and you feel nearly whole
and worth something other than
cheap laughs and sick jokes
and you feel like maybe
tomorrow
will
be
the
day
when
you
really
feel
right side in.

When you burn your journal from last year
when you were in love
with an untrustworthy weatherman,
then your plan to run away is
as real as it can get.

I let the last embers burn in the fireplace. They glow orange-red and they flake off and fly up the chimney because paper is light, but ash is lighter and Irenic Brown is lighter even, than paper and ash and everything that doesn't matter.

When you burn your journal, it's easy to forget things. It's easy to forget people. If Stanzi and Gustav don't come back, then I won't miss them, same as I won't miss my mother and her basement of pain and I won't miss Lansdale and her fauxkemia and I won't miss the bomb threats and I won't miss English class behind the lilac bushes in the corner parking lot where we discussed Oliver's "Goldfinches" and its themes and meanings way too much because it was *on the test last year*.

I miss Shane.

He's already burned his journals.

He never told anyone, either.

We keep each other's secrets.

It's time for us to be together for real. Even if we sleep on the streets. Even if we don't have anything to eat. Even if we end up coming back here. It's time for us to be together.

Stanzi—Thursday—Kenneth

IN THE PLACE OF ARRIVALS

Gustav sits in the pilot's seat until the blades stop rotating. He takes off his headset and smiles at me. Then he climbs out of the helicopter and comes around to my side and opens the invisible door and helps me out and onto the not-invisible grass.

Solid ground.

I have no idea where we are. I ask, "Do you know where we are?"

He answers, "We're exactly where we're supposed to be. I promise."

We look at each other, and I can see that something has changed inside Gustav. He's more than just a boy building a helicopter. He's a man who flew a helicopter. I hug him, and it's not the kind of hug I'd give China or Mama; it's the kind of hug I'd give Wolfgang if I was Stanzi. I can hear Gustav breathing the smell of my hair into himself. I can feel him relax in my arms. I want to kiss him again. I'm about to when a woman walks out from the brush to our right.

"Welcome!" she says.

She's dressed in a pair of dirt-covered stonewashed jeans and a sweatshirt. Her hair is pulled back into a ponytail, and it's going gray at the sides. There is no doubt that she can see the helicopter.

Gustav says, "Are you Patricia?"

She nods.

"Nice to meet you." Gustav shoves his hand toward her and she shakes it. She looks as if she could cry for a month. I have no idea why.

"I'm Stanzi," I say. "This is Gustav."

"You know Kenneth?"

Both Gustav and I look perplexed. This causes her to look more concerned than happy. She glances behind her every five seconds or so—as if she's checking to see if she's been followed.

She looks at the helicopter. "You have to hide it," she says. "Or else they'll destroy it."

"Where could I hide it?" Gustav asks. "It doesn't fit anywhere else."

She thinks in her head. She talks to herself. She is like a person who has split in two. "They don't come up here anymore. They won't see it. Maybe we can leave tomorrow. Maybe we can leave tonight."

"Leave?" Gustav asks. "I'm sorry. I'm out of fuel."

She says, "You are?"

I turn to him. "You are?"

"I am. Completely. Had we not found this perfect field, we would have crashed."

At the word, my body shivers.

Stanzi—Thursday—
Stanzi Takes a Test

IN THE PLACE OF ARRIVALS

There's a test. I took it on the Internet a few times. It's a yes-or-no test. There are no ovals. There are no right answers. The test is wrong, so all your answers are wrong if you have to take the test. It is a lose lose situation.

The first question on the test is: *Have you or has a loved one experienced or witnessed a life-threatening event that caused intense fear, helplessness, or horror?*

There are twenty-three other questions.

If you answer yes to any of them, you are supposed to tell your doctor.

I think about the first question. *Have you or has a loved one experienced or witnessed a life-threatening event that caused intense fear, helplessness, or horror?*

This is a test for PTSD—post-traumatic stress disorder.

As far as I'm concerned, everyone is a witness. As far as

I'm concerned, if anyone says they're not, they are lying worse than Lansdale Cruise. As far as I'm concerned, this first question reads like one of China's poems.

Your PTSD Test Has More Self-Esteem Than I Do

Have you
or has a loved one
experienced
or
witnessed
a
life-threatening event
that caused intense fear,
helplessness,
or horror?

We are still standing in the perfect field with Patricia. She says, "The whole world causes me intense fear, helplessness, and horror."

I say, "You should tell your doctor." Then I stare at her as if she is untrustworthy. Mind readers are slippery.

"Not always," she says.

Gustav is too busy unloading a few things from the helicopter to hear this or understand that Patricia, like the dangerous bush man, can read minds.

I'd like to ask Patricia what Gustav thinks of me.

"He loves you," she says.

"Shhh," I say. "He can hear you."

"Only if he's listening."

We watch him rifle through a box. He finds the quality letter *P* from the dangerous bush man and hands it to her.

She says, "Can you take me to him?"

Gustav and I look at each other and shrug.

"Kenneth," she says, and holds up the *P*. "You know him? He made this for me." When neither of us answers, she says, "Fuel. We must get fuel."

Stanzi—Thursday—
Hikers Lost

IN THE PLACE OF ARRIVALS

Patricia takes us to her house. It's a tree house. A real house in the trees. Inside the tree house, there are three pianos.

A man greets us, and Patricia introduces him as Gary. Gustav doesn't say anything. I tell Gary that my name is Stanzi and that he has curious bone structure.

"Curious how?"

"Your mandible is displaced," I say. "Did you never notice that?"

Patricia looks somehow pleased that I have said this. The man, Gary, seems annoyed.

Gustav asks, "Do you have any food?"

Patricia speaks before Gustav can say any more. "They were hiking. Got lost. How long did you two say you've been walking around hungry?"

I can see Gustav processing, but slowly. I say, "Almost

three days. Lost the trail and then I swear we went in circles for two days." I don't know why I'm lying.

"We didn't," Gustav snaps. "I knew where I was going." I don't know why Gustav is lying, either.

"Well then how did we end up here?" I ask.

I'm impressed by our acting skills. A physicist and a biologist.

"You're just impatient," he says. He smiles slightly when Gary isn't looking. Gustav knows I avoid confrontation. Gustav probably knows everything, but we never talk about it.

"I was hungry, Gustav. My sister must be worried sick!" I look at Patricia and Gary. "Do you have a phone I could use to tell her we're okay?"

Gary hasn't smiled yet. He says, "There are no phones."

"Oh," I say.

Gustav looks like he's about to say something real when his actor says, "Where are we?"

Gary takes Patricia by the arm and leads her into another room of the tree house and closes the door. I look at Gustav and smile. He says, "He doesn't like us."

"I don't think he likes anyone."

"I expected a real welcome," he says. "I didn't think we'd have to lie."

"I don't like lying," I say.

"She said they'd destroy it. I just spent nine months building it. They can't destroy it. Why would they destroy it?"

"I don't know," I say.

"She seems nervous. Too nervous," Gustav says. "So far, this doesn't seem like a hotbed of genius." He's shaking a little.

"Are you nervous?" I ask.

"I'm hungry," Gustav answers. "I need fuel."

"There are no departures," I say. "That's what the bush man told me. He said, *There are no departures, but I left and look at what happened to me.*"

"He's dramatic," Gustav explains. "Remember the lemonade?"

"But he wasn't being dramatic. It's written on the map."

"Join us for brunch!" Gary says, exploding from the door, grinning. Patricia walks behind him and looks as if he stole her smile and took it for himself. She is expressionless, though anyone with a heart can see she's afraid.

"Thank you!" Gustav says. I believe this is the first time I've ever heard Gustav use a vocal exclamation point. "Will anyone at brunch have a phone? Stanzi should really call her sister."

I put on my actor's face. My worried-and-need-to-call-my-sister face.

It's at this moment I feel inexplicably happy.

I'm not gathered around the holly bush talking about dominant and recessive genes. I'm not drawing any Punnett squares. I'm not trying to explain to the class the magic of transcription and translation of DNA so they can better prepare for the tests.

I don't even miss it.

In two days of flying I forgot about it completely, as if it never existed.

I like this better, whatever it is. Whatever it isn't.

The Interviews II—
Thursday

The man and the cameraman wake up in their adjoining hotel rooms and are relieved that the earthquake has stopped. The hotel restaurant is empty for breakfast service. The man orders an English muffin, and when it comes out sliced and not fork-split, he has a fit the size of Saskatchewan.

Interview #1 Rosemary P. Hatfield (Health III)

The man notes how long her legs are and wonders where she gets pants that fit. She notes that he has really annoying hair and wants to ask how much hair product he had to put in it to make it look that way.

"Do you know anything about the helicopter?" the man starts.

"Helicopter?" she says. "You're in the right wing, but physics is up the hall a few doors."

The man notices a poster on the wall. The poster says: 40%
OF PREGNANCIES ARE UNPLANNED.

Rosemary sees him reading it and says, "More and more of my students get pregnant and have no fucking idea how it happened."

"Um," the man says. He gestures toward the recording camera.

"What? Oh. I said *fuck*, didn't I? Shit. I forgot."

"It's just FCC policy. Do you want to start over?"

"Can't you just bleep it out?"

"I guess. I just thought—uh—that you might want to seem more—uh..."

He indicates for her to continue. She looks back at the poster.

"I have this one board member. Never had kids. Says he knows about *the kids of today*; suggests I teach about abstinence only. Blow his ass up.

"I have the gaggle of overprotective parents who refuse to let their kids watch the childbirth video. Blow their asses up.

"I have a math teacher who says it's not my place to teach kids how to stay safe from sexually transmitted diseases. Whose job is it? Hers? Because their parents sure as hell aren't teaching them shit. Blow them all up.

"Do you think I went to college thinking I'd need to be armed to teach kids about herpes?" she asks. "If I wanted to shoot bad guys, I'd have been a cop."

The man motions to the cameraman to keep rolling.

She says, "My dad was a cop. He was made of glass."

She says, "Best people in the world are made of glass. You can see right through glass. You can trust it."

She stops talking and goes to her desk drawer and grabs her purse.

She points to the clock. "You guys ready for the drill?"

The man and the cameraman shrug.

"Here it comes."

The alarm sounds. The students file out. The teachers file out, lessons in hand, ready to teach outdoors if they have to. As the man and the cameraman walk past the office on their way out the door, the cameraman turns and walks backward, camera rolling, and captures the dogs and the police entering the building.

The principal is the last one to leave. She is the captain of the ship. She says, "How will I ever achieve anything?"

Interview #2 Lansdale Cruise

"You again," she says.

"I wondered if you could explain what you know about the helicopter," the man says.

"I know a lot about the helicopter."

"Great."

"How old are you?" she asks.

The man says he's thirty-nine.

"Does that mean you're forty-five, or are you really thirty-nine?"

"I can show you my ID if you want," he offers.

The cameraman says "Jesus Christ" under his breath.

Lansdale Cruise says, "You're kinda cute. You married?"

"Nope."

"Thirty-nine?"

"Can we get back to the helicopter, please?" the cameraman says.

"Sure," Lansdale says. "What about it?"

"Was it real?"

"Didn't it fly them out of here?" she says.

"Did it? Are you sure they didn't just hop on a bus or a train or something?"

"They flew in the helicopter. Gustav built it. It took him many months."

"And could you see it?" the man asks.

"Yes. Every day of the week."

"Does that mean no?"

"Can I say on the record that my latest stepmother is a lying bitch and I hate her? If I say that, will it get on air?"

"Probably not."

"I guess it's a bit off-subject," she says.

"So you couldn't see the helicopter?"

"Why are you so hung up on the damn helicopter?" Lansdale asks.

"We're trying to figure out where the missing kids are."

"The missing kids are fine. Gustav knows what to do. Have you interviewed the bush man yet? He'd be the guy to ask."

"Really? I didn't think he was real."

"When you find him, make sure you ask him for his special lemonade. It's delicious," Lansdale says.

Then she walks away.

Interview #3 Random male student in parking lot

The man says, "Do you know where I can find the bush man?"

The student says, "What are you talking about?"

"What do you think about the helicopter?"

The student, who is getting into his car, replies, "The helicopter is the only way out."

Interview #4 China Knowles

China is still inside out. She is no longer a tongue. She is now an anus. These are never China's best moments. People are very uncomfortable about anuses, and yet everybody has one. It's complicated.

"Do you know where I can find the bush man?" the man asks.

China/anus nods.

"Can you show us?"

The anus contracts and runs away on China's legs. The man and the cameraman try to keep up, but they soon realize that China Knowles is not taking them to the bush man but is running away from them.

Interview #5 Stanzi's parents

"We have to be somewhere before five," the father says.

"I won't keep you long. Can we come in?"

The mother answers. "No."

"Okay."

"Are you worried about your daughter?"

The two of them stare at him. They look unstable. "Which one?" the mother asks.

"You have another daughter?"

"Yes."

"We didn't know that."

"Well then, you're a very lazy reporter."

The father starts to cry. The cameraman zooms in on this.

"We have to be somewhere," the mother says, and pushes the camera out of the way, and they walk hand in hand down the sidewalk.

The man is sweating. The cameraman films a bead of sweat dripping from the man's forehead down his cheek and his neck.

Interview #6 Chick's Bar

The man and the cameraman walk into a bar. All the people in the bar climb under their tables. Those on stools somersault over the bar and hide behind it. Nobody moves until the two men are gone.

Interview #7 Gustav's father

"I don't know this bush man."

"He makes lemonade?"

Gustav's father looks perplexed and then enlightened. "You're talking about Kenneth!"

"His name is Kenneth?"

"Kenneth has been to where Gustav and Stanzi are!"

"Stanzi? We heard her name was _____."

"We call her Stanzi. She calls herself Stanzi."

The man nods at this.

Gustav's father says, "We're very proud."

"Proud?"

Gustav's father asks, "Why wouldn't we be proud? Our boy built a helicopter. A helicopter! Do you have any kids?"

"No."

"Then you wouldn't understand."

"Can you point us toward this Kenneth?" the man asks.

"He's very private."

"I'm sure he won't mind. He'll be on national TV."

"He hates the television," Gustav's father says.

"Can you give me his last name?"

"I don't think so."

"Does he live nearby?"

"Can you go now?" Gustav's father asks. "You're taking up too much space."

"I'm taking up too much space?"

"Yes. Go away."

Gustav's father closes the door gently in the man's face.

The man looks at the cameraman and mouths the word *asshole*. When the man turns his back on the cameraman, the cameraman mouths the word *asshole*. Then he says, "How about we knock on some doors and ask where Kenneth lives?"

The man says, "I don't do that shit anymore. I'm national. Stories come to me, not the other way around."

161

China Knowles—Thursday Night—Fire Pit

I am China, the girl who swallowed herself, and I'd like to turn myself right side out again before I see Shane. I want him to see my skin. My eyes. My hair. I don't think I have particularly nice skin, eyes, or hair, but he might think so.

Maybe if he thinks so, I will, too.

Like a mirror.

People can be mirrors for other people. It happens all the time. Probably more than it should.

Burning my journal was fun, and I look around my room for anything else I should burn before I leave. I look through my desk drawers and my closet. I only find a stuffed monkey that Dad bought me when I was seven and he'd been on a business trip to San Diego. He showed me a lot of pictures from the zoo there.

It wasn't the same as going there with him.

I decide to burn the monkey, even though I have no particular animosity toward it.

Before I leave my room to go downstairs to light the monkey on fire, I see the one last reminder of the night that changed everything. The sweater. The sweater that he unbuttoned slowly at first, until I asked him to stop. The sweater missing its bottom three buttons. The sweater that has a tear in the last buttonhole. The sweater that acted like my mother's handcuffs.

It was my favorite sweater.

Mom found it in my trash can on trash day—a Friday—three days later—and told me that it cost her and Dad too much to just throw it away.

"You always loved it," she said.

"I don't want it anymore," I'd answered.

"Well... you don't just—I mean—I..."

Before she could see the missing buttons, I pulled it from the trash can and balled it up in my arms. "Forget it," I said. "I guess I do want it."

As I take it down the steps, I wonder what silk smells like when it's on fire. I look at the monkey's head, peering out from under my right arm, and I wonder what crazy chemicals will come out of it. For a minute I think about dressing the monkey in the sweater and then decide that the monkey should burn without shame. If nothing else, it's a good cover for my burning the perfect sweater in case Mom catches me. When I get to the living room, I decide that the fireplace is too small.

It's a cloudless night. I can see at least forty stars—even with our development's streetlight system. I can hear the music from Chick's Bar a block away. I can imagine adults there, bitching about their jobs and saying things like *Thursday is the new Friday.*

As I place the sweater and the monkey in the copper patio fire pit, there is a scream. It's a scream like someone has discovered a dead body. It's a scream like someone won the lottery. It's both kinds of scream.

It's coming from my basement.

I ignore it and I take a lighter to the monkey's tail and watch it burn.

Within seconds, I'm regretful about the monkey. Dad never meant to hurt me with those pictures and his stories about the zoo. I feel like a spoiled brat.

But as the sweater burns, I remember what a spoiled brat looks like.

What a Spoiled Brat Looks Like

The weatherman
makes weather, kneads
weather like a baker
kneads bread.
Once it's baked
it's no surprise
when he says
"Look! Bread!"

The weather he makes
is not good weather
for a picnic
or a ball game.
The weather he makes
is best for
staying indoors
and
staying quiet.

On his map it says
you were too ugly anyway.
On his map it says
you don't even have
a nice body.
On his map it says
I never liked you
and you smell weird.
Why are you crying?

I don't cry when I watch the sweater burn. Or I do cry,
but they are tears of relief. Shane knows these tears. We have
cried them together. When we meet, we clutch each other
like fledglings and we tweet out soft sobs about our spoiled
brats.

Shane's spoiled brat is a man old enough to be his father.

Shane's spoiled brat is in jail.

Mine is not.

○○○○●○

Irenic Brown asked me, when I was a rectum maybe four weeks ago as we passed in the hallway at school, why I hadn't killed myself yet. I didn't have an answer for him, and I don't have one now.

There's another scream. This time it's from behind me on the deck.

"What are you doing?" Mom screeches.

"I'm burning something," I say.

She squints into the fire pit. "Is that the monkey?"

"Yes."

She looks perplexed. She is wearing her latex bodysuit with chains and hooks. If I was normal I'd look perplexed, too.

"Do you need to talk about anything?" she asks.

"No."

"Your hair looks pretty," she says.

"Thanks."

"Okay," she says, as if she suddenly realizes that she's standing in plain sight on her development deck wearing nothing but a latex bodysuit. "I guess I'd better get back."

"I'm going to bed," I say.

"Good night."

"Good night."

When I get back to my room, I unpack the curling iron from my backpack and I pull out my phone. I set it so my ID is blocked.

And I dial Irenic Brown's number.

166

Stanzi—Thursday Night—
Hysterical Girl

IN THE PLACE OF ARRIVALS

Gustav and I are still acting. He plays the part of the boy who got us lost and needs directions. I play the part of the angry, scared girlfriend who wants to call home so no one worries about me. Patricia started this. We're just following her lead.

They feed us scrambled eggs. Duck eggs. They feed us stale bread. They feed us homemade pickles that survived the winter.

Gustav and I pretend to nap all afternoon because we are playing parts and we said we hadn't slept in three days, so we figured we should be tired.

But Gustav doesn't sleep because Gustav never sleeps.

I don't sleep because Gustav isn't sleeping.

We lie on our sides and stare at each other. We don't say a word, but the whole time I tell Gustav I love him in my brain and I can feel him doing the same. Then we lie on our backs and hold hands while we stare at the ceiling. I think about how Patricia wants to leave here. I think about how she told me Gustav loves me.

I try to remember how many people I saw when I was in the dining hall. It's like counting sheep before bed. One sheep wore wild eyeglasses. One sheep was bald. One sheep was dressed in a Sunday suit. One sheep was missing part of his ear. One sheep had a lab coat on like mine. He didn't look like a good talker.

Gustav wakes me up for dinner.

"Did you sleep?" I ask.

"Sure," he says, but I know that means no.

"How do you function without sleep?" I ask.

"I sleep. Just a different way than you."

"I'm not hungry," I say.

"You're starving," Gustav says. "You're really worried about calling home and letting them know you're okay."

I take a deep breath.

"You're upset because no one has given us directions yet," he adds.

"I'm the hysterical girl and you're the quiet, brooding boy."

"We can't call attention to ourselves. They'll destroy the helicopter."

More drills.

Before I can say anything, Patricia knocks gently on our door and says, "It's time for dinner."

○○●○○

There are seventeen people here. When I wonder to myself if this is everyone, Patricia nods at me. When I wonder to myself if they are all going crazy from isolation, Patricia says, inside my head, *Only some of us.*

I eat as much as I can so I look the part of a hungry, lost traveler. Gustav is brilliant. He picks at his food and gains sympathy from the men, who shake their heads in solidarity as I prod him to ask them for directions to a phone to call home.

Gary explains, "We don't *want* directions. Why would any of us want to leave?"

I wonder if it's possible for Gary to be more smug than he already is.

Patricia says, inside my head, *Totally possible.*

I wonder, *Does everyone here read minds?*

No, she says inside my head. *Just me and Kenneth.*

Gary makes his smug lips form smug words. The words arrive in the atmosphere in smug word bubbles and say, smugly, "You, my dear, have found yourself in paradise and you don't even recognize it. Imagine finding Eden and not knowing it!"

I decide to avoid anyone who ever starts any sentence with "You, my dear" for the rest of my life.

Patricia says, "I want to introduce you to Marvin before our walk."

I say, "Okay."

Inside my head, she says, *Marvin is our biologist. I think you'd like his lab.*

When she says this, I wonder if I should take off my lab coat so I look more like the part I'm playing, but the thought of removing it makes my heart rate increase and my hands shake.

Inside my head, Patricia says, *Marvin thinks everyone is stupid. You won't need to change your clothes.*

○○○●○

Marvin wants to show me his lab. He walks me around and points to things.

Patricia sits in the corner of Marvin's laboratory, scribbling notes of some sort. Marvin takes me to his desk and shows me drawings. He tells me he has found two new organs in the human body.

"How?"

"How what?" he asks.

"How have you found new organs? Do you have cadavers?"

"People have died. This is biology, no?"

"You cut up your friends?"

"I'm the world's leading biologist. I can cut up whomever I please."

I want to tell him I've never heard of him, but I stay quiet as he shows me diagrams of his newfound organs. One is a small, glandular-looking thing. No bigger than a petit pois pea seed. He has it drawn between the third and fourth fingers of the right hand—between the knuckles.

"Does it also exist on the left hand?" I ask.

"No."

"Were all of your specimens right-handed?"

"Yes."

"Are there any left-handed people here?"

He looks at Patricia. She says, inside my head, *Don't remind him.* She says aloud, "Don't expect me to drop dead anytime soon, Marvin. Not gonna happen."

"It doesn't matter which hand," Marvin says. "What matters is what it does."

I look at him, waiting.

"Do you want to guess?"

"No."

"Why do you wear that coat and act stupid?" he asks. "You don't think any of us really believe you got here by hiking, do you?"

I stare at him. "What does it do?" I ask.

"If massaged for long enough, in the correct direction, and using the correct amount of pressure, that little pea can increase sex drive up to one thousand percent."

"Sex drive?"

"Yes," Marvin says proudly. "While millions of people buy dumb little pills for billions of dollars a year, they are unaware they have their own, personal pill right there," he says, pointing to his hand. *"Right there!"*

I look at Marvin blankly.

"So maybe you don't care about sex drive," he says. "But I have *cures.*"

I continue to look at Marvin blankly. Patricia continues to scribble left-handed in her small notebook.

"I've cured two types of cancer," Marvin brags. "Don't look at me like that."

"What cancer?" I ask.

"Leukemia, for sure. Some lymphomas, possibly."

Mention of leukemia reminds me of Lansdale Cruise. She only says she has it, but she lies. There's already a cure for lying.

"If I was back in the real world," Marvin says, "stuck in some tiny lab, taking orders from some idiot from pharmaceutical or government, we would never move forward. There is too much money to be made in being sick."

"You don't go back?"

Marvin laughs. His hair even laughs. I can hear tiny gray chuckles.

"So the cure is stuck here and cancer patients are stuck there?"

"I wouldn't think of it as *stuck*."

Patricia hums something as she scribbles. We both look over at her. She stops humming.

I ask, "You said you discovered two organs. What's the other one?"

Marvin looks at me seriously.

"Don't you trust me?" I ask.

"You're always talking about going home and calling your sister. You lied from the minute you got here. You haven't earned my trust."

"I miss my sister," I say. This is not a lie.

"She will forget about you in time," he says. "Everyone will. No one remembers me. No one remembers Patricia."

In my head I say, *The bush man remembers Patricia.*

Inside my head Patricia says, *The bush man?*

"You're a genius, Stanzi. Do you know that?" Marvin asks.

"Yes."

"You couldn't be here if you weren't one."

"Okay."

"So what is it that you do in *your* laboratory that's so important?" he asks.

"I dissect things. Frogs, mostly."

"How quaint," Marvin says.

"The frogs aren't quaint. They're dead."

"You must be working on *something* other than dissecting frogs like a ninth-grade know-nothing."

Patricia tells me in my head to trust Marvin. So I tell him.

I say, "I think there's an organ that will relieve guilt in humans."

His hair stands at attention and listens to me through the frayed ends.

"Like your sex-drive gland, I think they're keeping it from us because—"

"Because guilt drives the real world, my dear. Very right," he says. "Just like sex drive. You know they still don't teach *doctors in med school* what the entire clitoris looks like? When we draw our diagrams, we draw but a tiny piece of a large, fascinating organ. Like drawing the hand as a stump with no fingers. Why do you think that is?"

I stare at him, not knowing what the answer is. Not wanting to discuss that sort of thing with Marvin.

He says, "It's just another way to control us, love. Especially you women. God! Let's control the hysterical women!" His hair screams like a hysterical woman: *OHMYGOD! OHMYGOD! OHMYGOD!*

Lansdale Cruise—Thursday Night—
The Next Mrs.

Everybody is gone. My friends Stanzi and Gustav crashed in a helicopter. My friend China spontaneously combusted in her own front yard. The newsman asked me to marry him after that second interview, but I said no.

Except that nobody is gone and Stanzi and Gustav didn't crash, and China can't spontaneously combust because that shit is bogus. And the newsman didn't ask me to marry him, but I said yes.

Except I'm not sure he heard me.

Mr. Cruise is out looking for the next Mrs. Cruise. I know this because she called the house phone earlier, very apologetic, and said she'd be late for their date. She told me to give him the message. I didn't.

China won't answer her phone.

Gustav and Stanzi have gone somewhere else, where they belong.

I have the thirty-nine-year-old news guy's card. It has an office number in Los Angeles. I looked up the area code of his cell number on the Internet and it's from Ohio. I wondered why he acted so Californian. It's because he's from Ohio.

He looks like he's been eating the wrong foods. He probably hasn't had a massage in years. He has a cheesy smile and uses too much hair product. He looks unloved. We're made for each other.

I burn and cut myself all night and then I take a saltwater bath.

Except really I go to the Hilton.

China Knowles—Thursday Night— *Fuenteovejuna*

"Hello?"

Irenic Brown's voice is smooth—a weather forecaster on a sunny day.

"Hello?" he says again.

I feel myself churning through the cycle. *Mouth, tongue, teeth, epiglottis, esophagus, stomach, duodenum, jejunum, ileum, cecum, colon, rectum, anus.* I skip the accessory organs because they are not useful to me. I have bile. I have gall. I know my liver is in there somewhere, but right now it's not useful to me. I have no filter.

"That you, AJ? Are you in a bathroom?" he asks. "Sounds gross."

I put on a different voice. I think of Lansdale and how well she lies. I make her part of my digestive system and I stop there, in my Lansdale canal, and say, "You wanna get some? I got a girl here wants some."

"Stop lying, AJ. You couldn't get a girl if you paid for one."

"She's out cold, bro."

"Who is this?" he asks.

"It's easier when they're out cold, right? Bitches fight too much."

"Wrong number," he says. Then he hangs up.

I look around my room and I plug my curling iron in. Just as it's getting hot enough, Mom knocks on my bedroom door and tells me to come out. I want to say, *Come out of what? My colon? My own mouth?* Instead, I unplug the curling iron and go downstairs.

●○○○○

Mom has put a bathrobe on over her black latex bodysuit and has asked her dungeon friends to leave. Dad is in bed because he has to fly somewhere else tomorrow to work. She sits me down at the kitchen table and tells me the police called her today about the bomb threats.

"They think it's you," she says.

"It's not me."

"So you know who it is?" she asks.

"It's not anyone."

She sighs and takes a hit off her electronic cigarette and she looks like a robot in a bathrobe. Shiny black exterior, glowing red electric drug. "It's got to be *someone*. The school isn't sending the threats to themselves."

"Maybe they are," I say. "I mean, metaphorically."

She looks at me and gives that worried, halfhearted smile.

"Maybe it's like *Fuenteovejuna*," I say.

"*Fuente* what?"

"*Fuenteovejuna*. The play about the town in Spain? In the fourteen hundreds?"

"What does this have to do with the police calling my house? Or you burning that nice monkey? Your father brought that home from a trip. He didn't mean any harm."

"Yeah. I regret burning the monkey."

"So?"

"*Fuenteovejuna* is a play, but it's about something that happened in real life in Spain in, like, fourteen-something. There was this commander in the town and he was out of control. He attacked innocent people all the time and raped women and stuff. He was so bad that they finally, as a town, agreed to kill him and bury him."

"I can't see how this relates, China."

"That's because you didn't let me tell you the end."

She motions for me to tell her the end.

I say, "Someone told Isabella and Ferdinand about his murder, so they sent out the magistrate to interrogate the villagers in Fuenteovejuna. No matter how many people they tortured—men, women, and even children—everyone had the same answer about who killed the commander."

"And?" Mom takes another drag off the robot cigarette.

"And they all answered the same way," I say. "They said 'Fuenteovejuna did it.'"

"Isn't that the name of the town?"

"Yes."

"So the town killed the commander?"

"Yes."

She stares at the sink, where there are two sex toys drying on the dish rack. My little sisters believe these are cooking utensils because one time she left them there until morning and we lied and told them that.

She says, "But the town didn't kill him, did it? The villagers were covering for the real killers, right?"

"Depends on how you look at it," I say.

"So what am I supposed to say to the detective when he calls back tomorrow?"

"You should tell him Fuenteovejuna did it. I bet he never read Lope de Vega. He'll probably go looking for some Latino-Irish guy named Fuente O'Vejuna."

"It's not funny."

"It's the truth."

I'm a throbbing organ on legs since I heard Irenic Brown's voice. I'm sweating. I feel like I could spontaneously combust.

Mom says, "You're not yourself lately."

I say, "Did you notice?"

"I figured you would tell me in time."

"I probably will."

I get up as she's taking another hit off the robot cigarette. "Us parents. We think we should do something."

"About what?"

"The bomb threats." She looks at me sideways. "Is there anything else we should do something about?"

"Do you think I learned about *Fuenteovejuna* in school?"

"I guess."

"Do you think the test makers know of *Fuenteovejuna*?"

"What test makers?"

"The ones sending the bomb threats. Those test makers."

"So you *do* know who's sending the threats?"

I stand at the doorway and sigh. "Yes."

"It's the test makers?"

"Sure."

"Do you think they're on the voice mail menu? I'd love to call and give them a piece of my mind."

"I don't know," I say. "But I'm tired and I have to go to school tomorrow. I'm going to bed."

When I get back to my room, I don't plug in the curling iron. I block my number and redial Irenic Brown's number. I wait until he answers and I make a noise like a police siren until he hangs up.

Stanzi—Thursday Night—Genius Debriefing

IN THE PLACE OF ARRIVALS

Marvin asks me where I think the missing guilt organ is. I show him the spot just at the base of my neck, above my clavicle, but near the shoulder. He presses on his and closes his eyes. I stand, waiting for him to tell me what he thinks, but he just stays that way, pressing my theoretic organ in his neck, and Patricia says, inside my head, *Let's leave him to figure it out.*

As we walk up the path I say, "But *I* wanted to figure it out. I wanted it to be *mine.*"

"His discoveries are trapped here, like he is," she says.

"It's *my* discovery."

"And you'll take it back to the world when you leave."

"Leave?" I say. "Why do you keep talking about leaving? There are no departures."

We walk quietly for a moment.

"So no one believes our story about hiking?" I ask.

"No."

"There must be other ways to get here than a helicopter."

She smiles. "It isn't just a helicopter. You know that."

"Gustav told me this place would be a hotbed of genius," I say.

"More like a vacuum of genius," she says.

I look to see if she's joking, but she's dead serious. I say, "Gustav said this is an invisible place. It doesn't seem invisible to me."

"I feel more invisible every day I live here," she says. "So will you."

I think about the drills. Patricia says in my head: *Yes. Just like the drills.*

"Is that why the bush man left?"

She laughs. "Why do you call him that?"

"Hard to explain," I say. "He's a good guy, but he scares people."

"Don't we all?"

I picture the dangerous bush man in my head: naked, trench coat, letters. I wonder if she can see him.

"I can see him."

I picture the bush, the lemonade stand, and the kisses.

"What's normal, anyway?" Patricia asks.

"It's not this place," I say.

We walk quietly again for a minute. The hill is steep. I wish the trees would help me breathe, like Mama always said they would.

"Tonight you and Gustav will be debriefed," Patricia says.

"Okay."

"They'll ask you things about the real world."

"Okay."

"They'll ask if you know Kenneth," she says. "You can't tell them the truth."

"Okay."

"I'm going to pretend I have my period and stay home," she says.

"Why?"

"I don't like debriefings," she says.

I wonder if the dangerous bush man was ever debriefed.

"He was. But he lied about us being in love."

"You're in love with the bush man?" I ask.

"Very."

"I thought you were married to Gary," I say.

She laughs. "Ha!"

I wonder if the bush man was like Gustav when it came to love.

"Exactly the same," she says. "Never knew what to do with his hands."

"He's a very good kisser," I say.

"Yes," she answers.

"He has the answers," I say.

○○○●○

Gustav is sitting high in a tree. I wave to him and he waves back. Patricia has gone to bed early because she has Lansdale Cruise cramps.

As Gustav climbs down, he says, "They told me they never believed our story because of your lab coat. *Who goes hiking in a lab coat?* they asked."

He mutters to himself as he descends the final two branches and jumps to the ground in front of me.

"They're very smart," I say. "Trying to turn you against me."

"Do you know where we are?" Gustav asks. "Do you know what this is?" He's talking like Gary now. He has smug up to his knees.

"I have a guess, but I don't trust what they've told you."

"We're in the smartest zip code in America," he says. "No one here has an IQ under a hundred and seventy."

"We're not in a zip code, Gustav. They don't get mail here," I say.

"Who needs mail? I never got mail at home. Why would I need it here?"

"You called it a zip code. It's not a zip code," I say. "Also, they already knew we weren't hikers. It had nothing to do with my coat."

He's agitated. I wonder what it's like having a helicopter to build every day for months and then not having anything to do.

"They told me they would have believed us if it wasn't for you," he says.

"They lie better than Lansdale Cruise. Marvin told me. Patricia told me. There's no other way to get here except the helicopter," I say. "And no way out, either, except the bush man got out."

"Kenneth," he corrects.

"Yes. Kenneth."

"He got out. He told me how to get out. Except the fuel. He never told me about the fuel," he says.

"You didn't tell *them* this, did you?"

"No."

"What's so great about a bunch of people with high IQs, anyway?" I ask. "Look at Gary. He may be smart, but he's a jerk."

Gustav says, "Smart people often have social issues. It's how we're made."

"We?"

"You have social issues," he says. "I have social issues. So what?"

"So neither of us are jerks," I say.

He says he needs a minute. "It's hard to catch up. All this new information," he says.

"We lied from the minute we got here," I say. "They don't trust us."

"Patricia lied."

"But then we lied, too," I say.

"I just went along with it," he says.

"Maybe we're not as smart as we thought we were," I say. "Maybe we're easily swayed. I don't know. But I don't like this place. I've been here for half a day and I don't like it."

Gary whistles to us like we're dogs. It's time for the genius debriefing.

"I'm going to tell them about the drills," I say.

186

"I'm going to tell them who's been sending the bomb threats," Gustav says.

I take a deep breath. "There is no way you can know this, Gustav. Scientifically, you don't have enough evidence," I say.

We walk toward the building where the dining hall is. As we walk, Gustav reaches over and touches my hand. I pull my hand away. Today has made me edgy. I wanted to come here. But now I don't want to be here. Gustav wanted to come here and then leave, but now he wants to stay. We are two very confused arrivals.

"It's China," Gustav says. "She's untrustworthy."

I'm glad we're not holding hands. I shout, "Where are you getting your information? Are you eating what insects eat?" Gustav looks shocked. I don't think I've ever yelled at him before. "China is your friend. She deserves more from you!"

Gustav stops on the path outside the building and looks down. "I apologize. You're right."

"She's the smartest zip code you ever met," I say.

"I wish sometimes that I had her words," Gustav says.

"No, you don't," I argue. "Because then no one would believe you, and people would call you untrustworthy because of bad luck. If you had your own words, it might be different. China can't win. She can only eat herself."

"You know what happened, don't you?"

"I know."

"Will she ever recover?"

"Do any of us ever recover?"

"I don't know," he answers.

"Did she ever tell you about Fuenteovejuna?" I ask.

"No."

"When we get back, she will."

"Get back?" he asks.

○○○●○

There are several rooms inside. It's like a church, but with no god. In the room with Gustav and me are sixteen people. Marvin is here, no longer pressing on his/my theoretical guilt-free gland; Gary is here in his fog of smug. The others are all names I never even hear. They introduce themselves by telling us only what they do and where they learned how to do it. *Physics, MIT; biology, UCLA; music, Berklee; neuroscience, Penn; law, Harvard; poetry, NYU; economics, Yale; abstract painting, Royal College of Art, London; architecture, Cornell; master chef, Culinary Institute Lenôtre; mathematics, Stanford; psychology, MIT; philosophy, Harvard; botany, Trinity; astronomy, Cambridge; chemistry, Cornell.* After the introductions, we're supposed to be impressed, I think.

I'm not.

Gustav is probably not, either.

They ask us about our daily lives. We tell them that we don't watch television but that most people do and that it's not all bad, though most of it is. We tell them we don't care about fashion or culture, and I point at my lab coat as an example. We tell them about the wars we're in and I tell them about the war in Congo and they seem uninterested. They are similarly uninterested in the drug cartels in Mexico and the wars in the Middle East, one of them snorting at Gustav's mention of Syria, and they are not at all interested in the tsunamis, the hurricanes, or the earthquakes. Not even the one that caused a nuclear reactor to melt down.

They ask us about the Internet.

Gustav says it is informative and a marvel.

I add that it causes pain and is filled with pornography. The room laughs at this. The whole room jiggles its belly.

"Don't you have the Internet here?" Gustav asks.

"We *are* the Internet here," Gary replies. The room jiggles again. The walls laugh. The lighting fixtures make a clinking noise.

"Well." Gustav stops to choose his words well. "You can't know everything the Internet knows."

Gustav and I bounce around like the Ping-Pong balls in a lottery machine. We are in a genius bouncy house. The sixteen residents still sit in their chairs, but we are thrown and sprung from floor to ceiling to wall until they contain themselves.

As I float from surface to surface, I want to dissect all of them. Find their livers. Dehydrate them. I wish I had my *Dealing with People You Can't Stand* book that Mama and Pop bought me for Christmas.

Gustav has blood running down his face when we land. He wipes it with his finger and checks to see if it is blood or sweat. It's both. I take a tissue from my lab coat pocket and press it on the small cut above his right eyebrow after gently wiping his forehead of the layer of frustrating sweat. It's been an hour.

They ask about school. We tell them about the drills.

One asks, "Every day? The alarm goes off every day?"

"Yes."

"And you go outside?"

"Yes," Gustav answers. I think of him under his black walnut tree. I remember that we're resilient weeds. I look at the sixteen others. I don't know what they are.

"We have to do our tests there," I say. "Even if it's raining."

"It's just water," Marvin says.

Another says, "I'm sure you pass them. You're both competent."

"The tests aren't for us," Gustav says. "They're for them."

I add, "For assessment."

I hear Gustav's thoughts in my head. *Just like now. We're being assessed.*

"Who makes these assessments?"

"A company," Gustav says.

The sixteen of them stare at us. We stare back at them. One of them presses a button on his chair and a wall drops down between us.

Gustav says, inside my head, *They can probably still see us. Just sit there.*

I say, "Okay."

He says inside my head, *You can hear what I'm thinking?*

I think *yes*, but he doesn't hear me. So I whisper, "Yes."

He looks concerned, so I say, "Don't worry. I won't pry."

We sit for three minutes. Gustav talks to me in my head as we sit.

He thinks: *These people aren't exceptional. They're cowards.*

I want to ask Gustav about fuel, but they can probably hear me through their secret genius wall, so I keep looking ahead. I fold my hands on my lap as if I was in a photographer's studio in a shopping mall. We wait.

Gustav says inside my head, *Kenneth told me I was going on a mission. I didn't know what kind of mission, but any mission was better than testing week. I thought this would be different. Maybe it is. Maybe we belong here. Maybe we don't. I can't tell yet.*

A click sounds and the wall lifts.

Gary is standing up and the other fifteen are still sitting.

Gary says, "Where's the helicopter?"

Gustav answers before I can say anything. "We crashed."

"Where?"

"Three days from here. I don't know what direction," Gustav says. "Remember when we said we'd been walking for days? When we arrived?"

"You have no wounds to indicate a crash," Gary says.

"The trees," I say, thinking of Mama. "The trees saved us. Though I did twist my ankle climbing down, and Gustav got a small bump on his head from the impact."

Gustav rubs the side of his head.

Gary contemplates. He says, "Our first job is to recover it. We'll start searching tomorrow."

I hear Gustav trying to find a way to ask if they'll destroy it, but before he can say anything, one of the others presses the button and the wall drops down again.

Gustav and I sit there and stare ahead. I whisper, "They're

going to destroy it. I know it. We have to get out of here." Gustav nods as if he might believe me.

When the wall recedes into the ceiling again, the sixteen geniuses are gone. The room is empty. Gustav looks at me and holds out his hand. I take it and we leave through the front door, which opens as we approach it and closes behind us.

Outside, there is a message meticulously hand-lettered on wood.

It says, in red paint, THERE ARE NO DEPARTURES.

For Stanzi: Reset. Reset. Reset. II

There is a tiny hole
and if you unbend a paper clip
and insert it into the hole,
the world resets.
It becomes a walk
to the bus station in
the middle of the night
when even the bush man
is sleeping.
It becomes a safe place for
people
like
you

because the monsters
are getting
required
amounts of rest
for testing day.

I try not to run. I try to maintain control. Guts on the inside, me on the outside.

I am new.

I didn't leave a note for anyone, not even my sisters. I'll miss them, but now they can have Mom's attention and they won't have to share a room.

I text Shane and he says that he's sleeping at a friend's house in New York City and that I should call him when I get there. First bus leaves at 3:45 a.m. and arrives at six. I text back that I will be there at six. I write, "If you want to meet me at Port Authority, that would be cool." But I guess he turned his phone off because he doesn't reply.

The streetlights are a funny color. I never really noticed it before. They are a mix of amber and rose, and I feel like I'm walking through a field in the future. Maybe that's what will happen to our orderly suburban development. Maybe it will regenerate, like a liver. Maybe it will eat us up and swallow us and make us feel the acid as it breaks us back down into molecules.

Stanzi would know if that's possible.

I regret not leaving her a note. If she ever comes back, I want her to know I'm okay. She's smart and will probably know where I went.

I'm concentrating hard on staying right side out. With every step it becomes easier. I want to try talking out loud and look forward to getting to the station and purchasing my ticket so I can say "Good morning" to the cashier, so I can say "Hello" to my fellow travelers.

When I arrive at the station, a businessman walks in front of me when I'm clearly in view. I think he's going to open the door for me, but instead, he walks in himself and lets the door close behind him. I reach down and touch my forearm to make sure I'm here. It would be a shame to be invisible.

He's paying for his ticket at the counter when I walk in behind him.

I say, "Good morning!" and he and the cashier look at me as if I have said something dirty.

I don't swallow myself. Instead, I try, "Hello!"

The cashier looks at me and smiles the smile of a cashier at 3:35 in the morning. I might have just made his day a little better. I make a mental note about how this feels. It feels good to make a person's day a little better by saying something simple. I make a mental note to write a poem on the bus called "Things That Make Me Feel Good," but then it feels selfish to want to feel good.

As I buy my ticket, I wonder if the cashier feels guilty about whatever makes him feel good. As I go to the bathroom in the tiny bus station, I wonder if my mother feels guilty about her basement of pain, if my little sisters feel guilty about eating ice cream or cookies or whatever makes them feel good.

The bus arrives and as I hand my ticket to the driver he says, "Are you sure you're not supposed to be in school today?"

"I'm sure," I say.

He laughs like he wasn't serious. I laugh, too, and my mouth has trouble forming the shape of laughter.

I realize I haven't laughed in ages.

I think of Tamaqua de la Cortez and wonder why she can laugh. I think back to all of the ex-weathergirls. If Gustav was here he could graph the data. If Stanzi was here, she could give me the physiological reasons for laughter and the lack of laughter. If Lansdale was here, she would make me cookies and they would taste delicious.

"Are you getting on or not?" the businessman behind me asks. He even shoves a little, as if the bus will leave without him even though the driver is still outside closing the luggage doors on the side.

I stop cold and turn to him. "Did you just shove me?"

When we lock eyes, he seems genuinely sorry. When I was just the back of a girl, I deserved shoving. Now that I'm the front of a girl, I might be human, I guess.

He almost makes an apology. I can see it right behind his eyes. It's a banner like on those airplanes that fly above the beach in summertime. *I'm sorry…I'm sorry…I'm sorry….* Instead, he just makes the move-it motion with his hand.

I squeeze to one side of the completely empty bus aisle and let him go past me. Then, when he sits down and settles and the bus driver gets on and I look at the sixty other seats in the bus, I walk right up to him and point to the seat next to him.

"May I sit here?" I ask. I'm fully right side out now. It feels good.

"What?"

"May I sit here?"

"Can't you sit anywhere else?" he asks. "The bus is empty!"

I sit in the seat directly across from him. I retract the armrest between the seats and I put my back against the cool window, extend my legs, and stare at him.

Ten minutes later, he gathers his things and moves to another seat.

Five minutes after he settles, I move to the seat directly across from him and stare at him again.

This dance continues all the way to New York City. The businessman grows more and more annoyed. I stop staring long enough to write the poem.

Things That Make Me Feel Good

Looking at a stranger and seeing
everything about him
because he is
easier to read
than the instructions
to prepare a packaged pizza.
Knowing that when
they slice him into
even pieces,

inside they will find
a banner that reads
I'm sorry ... I'm sorry ... I'm sorry.

I look up to see the businessman staring at me this time.
I say, "It looks like it will be a lovely day!"
He says, "It's supposed to rain in the afternoon."
I say, "Isn't it always?"

Stanzi—Early Friday Morning— Fuel

IN THE PLACE OF ARRIVALS

In the middle of the night, something wakes me from deep sleep and a dream. It's Patricia. She's standing next to my bed, watching me sleep.

"I'm not watching you sleep," she whispers. "I need you. Get up."

I get up and slip my clothing on.

"Leave the coat," she says as I try to slip my warm, slept-in lab coat back over my clothes. "It's white. People will see us."

I know I can't leave the coat. She must understand because she waits as I remove my clothes and put the coat on, and then put my darker clothing back on top.

As we leave the tree house, she says, "We've been collecting fuel."

I'm still just coming out of REM sleep. I think, *We?*

"We've been waiting for this day."

"You waited for Friday?"

"We waited for the day we had a helicopter," she said. "It's my turn. We decided yesterday."

"You take turns?"

"The helicopter can only handle so much weight," she says. "We can't all go at once."

"I can see it on Tuesdays."

"I know."

"You can see it every day, right?"

"Yes."

"What about the others?"

"They can see it all the time, too. But they haven't found yours. Yet."

"How do you collect fuel?" I ask. But then I look at Patricia and I see she's crying and say, "I'm sorry."

She removes a small jar from the pocket of her Windbreaker, stops and holds the open jar to her cheek, and lets the tear drop in. Then she replaces the lid and continues to lead me through a forest far below where the genius village is.

I wonder if she knows that Gustav and I are all the helicopter will carry.

"It will carry exactly one hundred and forty pounds more," she says.

I wonder where our supplies will go.

"We can't fit any supplies."

I wonder if we will crash.

"We won't crash. I know you worry."

I wonder how she knows I worry.

"I know because it's in your face."

I wonder if I'm a human circulatory system, turning myself around over and over like China, my heart twisting in on itself.

"That's a strange thought. I don't know what that would look like."

I say, aloud, "It would look like a crash. Or a bomb. Or a school shooting. It would look like a note that says, *Gone to bed. TV dinner in freezer. Make sure you turn out the lights.*"

At this, Patricia stops again and retrieves her jar. She collects her tears and asks me if I want to cry and I tell her I never cry.

I tell her about my dream—the one I was having when she woke me up.

There were two coffins this time. There was a small one and a smaller one.

She says, "What does it mean?"

I answer her in my head. *It means it could have been worse.*

●○○○○

At the Place of Arrivals there is a magical spot. I don't believe in magic, so I can only guess that something geological or chemical has caused the magic. I'll ask Gustav in the morning. For now, I sit and watch as Patricia and two others, the law expert and the mathematics genius, collect their tears in jars. Nothing was said to make them cry. No one hit them. No one sent them a dissolution of marriage. No one gave them a standardized test. No one set off a bomb drill alarm. They simply arrived here at this spot and they began to cry.

I wonder the obvious—if tears fuel the helicopter.

"Not quite," Patricia says.

"I'm not sure what that means," I say.

"Well, how did you get here? Why did you leave? What made you come to a place you didn't even know existed?"

I think about this question for one hundred of their tears. I come up with many answers. *Boredom, freedom, the drills, the answers, the bush man, Gustav.*

Patricia says inside my head, *It had something to do with your dream, didn't it? The two coffins?*

"My parents take me to weird places on vacation," I say. "Sometimes the hotels have pools, but we don't swim, out of respect for the dead." I think of the dream and the two coffins—a small one and a smaller one. There is a feeling in my chest like someone is drilling.

The three of them cry for hours. After three full jars of tears are collected, secured, and buried, the four of us leave the area of crying. I'm relieved. I felt intense pain while I was there, but I didn't cry.

The mathematician and the law expert go in different directions. Patricia tells me to wait outside until she gets into the tree house. She tells me to count to one hundred. Before I get to fifty, the door opens and Gustav comes outside.

He says, "We'll leave tonight."

He says, "We'll take Patricia."

He says, "We'll have to make up our tests. Probably on Monday."

202

The Interviews III—
Friday

It's first light Friday morning. The man rolls out of the king-sized hotel bed and walks to the bathroom and urinates so loudly that he wakes the woman still under the sheets.

Interview #1 Lansdale Cruise

"Don't you like waking up early?" the man asks.

"No." She squints and then covers her head with the sheets again.

"Do you want to order room service?" he asks.

"No."

"The eggs Benedict here are delicious," he says. "Should I order you a plate?"

She says something but it's muffled by the sheets. He orders two plates of eggs Benedict and a pot of coffee from room service and then jumps on the bed until she finally pokes her head out.

"Fuck off!" she says.

"Oh, come on," he says.

She stares at him. *Oh, come on.*

"Don't be such a spoilsport."

"Spoilsport?" she says. "What are you, ninety? Nobody says that shit anymore."

"I do."

"Fuck off," she says again.

"Oh, come on," he says again.

She sits up with difficulty. Her hair is tangled around the pillows and has grown like creeper around the bed frame. As she unwinds it from around the bedside table lamp, she says, "Oh, come on? Isn't that what you all say?"

The man looks confused.

"How else would you get anything if not for *Oh, come on?*"

"You told me last night that you wanted to settle down," he says. "Remember?"

"And my hair is now ten feet longer than it was then, isn't it?"

Lansdale picks up her phone and takes a picture of the man in his underwear. She smiles. When breakfast comes thirty minutes later, she decides he is probably not the man she wants to marry. *He blows his nose in the shower and his hair is thinning. I could probably do better.*

Interview #2 The secretary at the high school

There is a sign on all entrances to the school. They read: NO ENTRY. TESTING IN PROGRESS.

The secretary will not let the man into the building. When he presses the buzzer on the intercom a third time, she stands up at her desk and mouths the words *Go away*. He holds up his press credentials.

"What do you want?" she asks, through the intercom.

"I was here yesterday and the day before. I'm doing a story about the missing kids."

"Somebody found them. Now go away."

"Somebody found them?" he asks. "I need to know more about this."

"Then read the damn newspaper," she says.

Interview #3 The old man at the convenience store

"Do you have a paper with the story about the missing kids being found?" the man asks. "I tried looking it up on the Internet on the way, but I couldn't find anything."

"I don't read newspapers," the old man says. "And I sure as shit don't look at the Internet."

The man picks up the local paper and starts to go through it.

"This ain't a library. You either buy it or you don't. *Then* you read it."

The man sighs.

The cameraman asks, as he films, "Do you know anything about Gustav or his helicopter?"

"I might," the old man answers.

"You know Gustav?" the cameraman asks.

"I know everyone," the old man says. "I'm the neighborhood know-everyone man."

The man puts the newspaper on the counter along with a dollar.

"It's a dollar thirty-five," the neighborhood know-everyone man says.

The man slaps down two quarters and goes out to the SUV. The cameraman stays and keeps rolling.

"Do you think Gustav built a helicopter for real?" the cameraman asks.

"That boy could build anything he wants. He's a genius."

"We've heard that. We've heard that _____ and Gustav flew away in a helicopter on Tuesday. Some people say they were invisible."

"Invisible? Naw. I saw Gustav fly over with my own eyes. Girl in the science coat was with him."

"So the helicopter is real?"

"But you can't see it," the neighborhood know-everyone man says. "Not unless you need to."

The SUV horn is loud. It makes the cameraman jump. He stops recording and holds the camera to his side.

"Thanks," he says. "I appreciate you talking to us."

"I wasn't talking to *him*," he says. "I was only talking to you."

The horn honks again.

"I apologize for his lack of patience. He's from LA."

"I heard he was from Ohio," the know-everyone man says.

When the cameraman gets back into the SUV, the man says, "I wanted to be back in LA by now."

"Why don't you give up on this story?" the cameraman asks. "It's not like we're actually getting anywhere."

The man says, "We should find that Kenneth guy. He can probably tell us everything."

Interviews #4, #5, #6 & #7 Kenneth's neighbors

The man asks, "Do you know where Kenneth lives?"

"Yes."

"Can you tell me?"

"No."

The man asks, "Do you know where Kenneth lives?"

"Yes."

"Can you tell me?"

"No."

The man asks, "Do you know where Kenneth lives?"

"Yes."

"Can you tell me?"

"No."

The man asks, "Do you know where Kenneth lives?"

"Yes."

"Can you tell me?"

"No."

Interview #8 China Knowles's mother

China's mother is dressed in a lavender velour track suit. "She's gone. Left this morning."

The man looks concerned. "Is she looking for her friends?"

"What friends?" she asks.

"Gustav? _____?"

"Oh. I doubt it. The police say she took the bus to New York City in the middle of the night."

"Do you think that's where Gustav and _____ are, too?"

"China was looking for a place to blend in. Those two were looking for a place to stand out," she says. "Is that camera rolling?"

"Yes," the cameraman says.

"Don't you have to ask permission before you film me?"

Just as the man begins to explain, she slams the door.

Interview #9 Stanzi's parents

Stanzi's mother opens the door and she is covered in blood. Stanzi's father stands behind her and he is holding a small stuffed rabbit.

"What happened?" the man asks.

Stanzi's parents answer, together, "What do you mean?"

"Has there been an accident?"

Stanzi's parents answer, "Yes. Yes."

The cameraman has his phone in his palm. "I'll call 911."

Stanzi's parents say, "It's too late for that."

"You clearly need help!" he says.

"Yes. Yes, we do," they answer. "But there is none."

The man inspects them and wonders if the blood is fake. He says, "Is that blood real?"

Stanzi's parents answer, "No blood is real blood unless someone cares."

Interview #10 The school principal

The man and the cameraman have parked the SUV in the faculty parking lot. They hope to catch a teacher willing to talk on the way to lunch.

A piece of macadam moves and shifts until a perfect circle of it lifts from the ground. The principal climbs out of the hole and when she stands in the lot, she brushes the dirt from her pantsuit and heads toward her car, three spaces from the hole.

The man says, "Can we talk to you once more about the missing kids?"

"Who are you?"

"We were in your office on Wednesday. Remember? We've spoken to several of your teachers, too."

"I have to get to lunch," she says. "It's testing day."

"Just two minutes?" the man says.

"Fine," she answers.

"Has anyone heard from them?"

"Who?"

"Gustav and _____," he says.

"No."

"What about the helicopter? Did your science department know he was building one?"

"Who?" she asks.

"Gustav. He built a helicopter."

"That's what you think."

"That's what everyone tells us."

"Not me."

The man flips through his notes. "That's true. When you talked to us last we were talking about the bomb threats."

"We haven't had one in two days. It's a miracle," she says.

"But we were here yesterday. The drill came as we talked to your health teacher."

"Rosemary?"

"Yes," the man says, checking his notes in his notepad.

"That woman puts condoms on bananas for a living. I wish I had it so easy."

"So you haven't had a threat today?"

"Not that I know of. I've been in my office. They removed my phone so we could fit more paper onto my desk."

"You don't have a phone?"

She looks at the man like he is stupid. "Who wants a phone when all it ever does is ring?"

Interview #11 A mother who's come to pick her son up from school

The woman is in workout gear, sitting in her car, which is parked in the pickup zone.

"I just got back from the gym. I look a mess."

"We won't take long," the man says. "Just a question about the school and some—"

When the woman opens her mouth, the story comes out in one long string. She doesn't even have to move her lips. She just opens wide, and her mouth is like a radio. "Someone sent a bomb threat to the school board meeting last night. It was spelled out on the assorted melon plate. It said, *Tomorrow*. The board debated what this could mean for forty-five minutes. Some thought it was a threat. Others thought it was a message from their respective gods to remind them of what power they have. Someone thought the melon cubes could have shifted in transit. Someone asked if the melons were American melons or imported. The meeting adjourned to a board member's house, where they were going to plan a trip to shoot turkeys with bows and arrows."

She closes her mouth.

The man asks, "Are you on the board?"

She says, "Oh, look! There's Henry now! Looks like the board was wrong! First day without a bomb threat since September."

As the kid gets into the passenger's seat he says to his mother, "You went on TV in your gym clothes?"

○○○●○

The man and the cameraman arrive back at the hotel, and the man goes directly to the bar and orders a double. The cameraman orders a soda. The police chief sits in the corner of the bar with four men from the school board. They're talking about shooting turkeys.

The man grows angry as he eavesdrops on the conversation. He tells the cameraman that he's going back to his room.

There he finds Lansdale Cruise freshening up at the vanity in the bathroom.

"You're still here?"

"It was testing day. You didn't think I was going to *that*, did you?"

"I'm busy now," he says. "You'll have to go."

Lansdale says, "My father beats me."

The man says, "I don't think that's true."

Lansdale says, "I'm the one sending the bomb threats."

The man says, "I don't think that's true, either."

Lansdale says, brushing a new lock of hair that has fallen in front of her face out of the way, "I've got superpowers. You'll see."

"You weren't that great of a lay," he says. He opens the door.

Lansdale gathers her things. On her way out the door she says, "You're not so great of a lay, either. Plus, your hair is thinning and your balls smell like dog shit."

China Knowles—Friday— Tidal Wave

I am China, right side in. I'm in New York City. Shane isn't answering his phone and he didn't meet me at Port Authority. The old me—a stomach, a colon, a rectum—might retreat now, but instead, I know I will find him if I look hard enough.

My mother has called me three times but I didn't pick up. Then she stopped. She texted to say the police know where I am. But I'm not a criminal, so I'm not afraid as I step onto the uptown A train. I'm not afraid as I step out of the subway station and walk up Broadway. I'm not afraid when I ring Shane's old door buzzer. I'm not even afraid when no one answers my buzz.

I buy a juice at the juice bar downstairs.

I say, "Give me something that tastes horrible."

She hands me a fresh beet and carrot mixture with some

seaweed in it. It's disgusting. I go to Central Park and find a bench.

Next to the bench is a trash can and I can hear it ticking, so I scoot closer and put my ear to it. The carrot/beet/seaweed juice is making my stomach turn. I feel my salivary glands working hard to keep things calm.

Tick tick tick tick tick tick.

What better place to die than here?

Your Ticking Bomb Has More Self-Esteem Than I Do

For one thing
it does not
have to
look at itself
in a mirror.
Or brush its hair
or its teeth.
Or maybe
when it does
if it does
it makes the ticking
louder
because it
can't stand itself,
either.
Maybe it's easy

to destroy things.
Maybe it's easy
to self-destruct.
Maybe your ticking bomb
is just faking it
and what it really
needs
is someone
to talk to.

I gulp down the beet/carrot/seaweed juice and my body
tells me to stop but I don't stop because my hand holds the
cup to my lips and I suck through the straw with no real idea
of why I'm forcing something inside me that I don't want
inside me.

This is the story of my life.

China: the girl who has things inside her that she doesn't
want inside her.

As I stand, Central Park wraps around my waist and I
grab both sides of the trash can, nine and three on the clock,
and I stick my head in so far that the ticking bomb must be
inches from my head and I vomit a dark pink mess.

It splashes up with each heave and spots of it land on my
glasses as I heave again and again. I vomit an ocean of juice. It
swirls in the trash can and becomes a loud, angry tidal wave,
and people in Central Park start to run in the opposite direction.

There is screaming.

I'm still stuck to the can—hands at nine and three. I'm

still heaving, but nothing else comes out. I feel it dripping from my chin as the wave rises above me higher than the Chrysler Building, and I have no place to hide. Either I will be washed away or I will not be washed away. The ticking is louder.

And so I jump right into the center of it. Right into the trash can, headfirst. Right into the vomit, into the bomb.

It's as pink and pulsing as my esophagus in here.

It smells like beets and beets smell like fresh earth, and it's all I can do to not stop and fill my mouth with dirt because it smells so like home, like playing with my sisters in the back-yard and building dirt castles for the ants and the ladybugs and the spiders. I want to eat that. I want to eat childhood and become childhood and become the mound of dirt and become my little sisters, who still don't know about anything except flannel pajamas and dolls and dumb shows like *Scooby-Doo!*

I travel through the red tunnel hands first, like I'm flying. I pass the bomb. It ticks like a metronome. It's keeping time for musicians in the Kaboom Orchestra. We are all musicians in the Kaboom Orchestra, only no one knows it yet.

I see trash, then, on every side of the red tunnel within the tidal wave. Sandwich wrappers. Used gum. A math test. Fifty coffee cups. Cigarette packs. A broken snow globe. A baseball hat. A half-eaten doughnut. A condom wrapper. A love note. A plastic medicine bottle with the prescription scratched off. A boy. There is a boy here.

At the bottom of the trash can, he is clinging to a piece of paper that is plastered across his chest. The paper says *Tick tick tick*.

"Are you okay?"

"Are you okay?"

"Are you okay?"

I open my eyes and I'm still standing at the trash can in Central Park. My hands are still at nine and three and I still have vomit dripping off my chin and speckling my glasses. The person asking me if I'm okay hands me a brown napkin and hurries on.

She probably hears the ticking.

I sit down on the bench and spit. Then I wipe my face and look down at my backpack and it has drops on it, too. So does my shirt. My sleeves. Everything I have is speckled with pink puke.

I move to another bench.

There is ticking in the trash can there, too.

So I move to another bench. And another. And another. I discover that all of the trash cans are rigged. Maybe they will explode at the same time. Maybe they won't.

I move to the other side of the bench where the ticking is less noticeable and then I turn myself upside down and sit with my feet in the air and my head in the caked dust that gathers under park benches.

There is no ticking when I am upside down. Everything is peaceful here.

I try Shane's phone again and it goes directly to voice mail. I haven't left a voice mail yet because I don't want him to think I'm needy. This time, since I'm safely upside down on a park bench in Central Park, I wait for the beep.

"Shane, it's China. I came to New York to be with you. I think we can make it if we're together, but I don't know where you are. I'm in Central Park just behind your building. I'll be upside down on a park bench and splattered in pink vomit."

As I watch people walk by—their shoes telling a different story each time—I inch closer and closer to the trash can side of the bench. But there is still no ticking while I'm upside down.

This means something, but I'm not sure what it is.

Lansdale Cruise—Friday Afternoon—
Oh, Come On

I wait behind the bush man's bush because he is the only friend I have left. I don't care about his answers or his letters this time. I don't even care about what's under his coat.

I want a conversation.

No one ever thinks the pretty girl wants conversation.

If I wrote poems like China does, I would write a poem about how no one ever thinks the pretty girl wants conversation, but I don't write poems. I bake, mostly.

This afternoon between the hotel and coming here to meet the bush man, I baked a batch of madeleines for him because I know he likes them and that's how I've been paying him for the answers.

Everyone thinks I pay him in other ways, but I don't.

I have never kissed the bush man. He likes to brush my hair. He likes me to lie so it grows right in front of him like

Hairnocchio. He likes to clip off the pieces that grow and tie them in braids and save them in a bag marked LANSDALE'S LIES and I don't mind because I know I lie. I'm not stupid. I just can't stop myself.

Last night at the Hilton I said I was eighteen. I said I like champagne. I said newsmen turn me on. I said I believe he grew up in Los Angeles when I know he grew up in Ohio. Last night I said I was once anorexic when I wasn't. I said I have leukemia, but it's in remission, which I don't and it isn't. I said that when I was seven, I sneezed for four days straight until they took me to the hospital, which I don't think is even possible. As the Ohio/Los Angeles man snored grossly beside me, I thought of hundreds of lies to make my hair grow so long that it would wrap him in a cocoon.

All that happened was that *I* was cocooned, not him.

And today, I'm tired of lying.

So I'm waiting to have tea with the bush man. He can have the last of my dishonest hair.

Stanzi—Friday—
Dumb Marvin

IN THE PLACE OF ARRIVALS

Because we're leaving today, Gustav tells me to act normal. So after breakfast, I go to Marvin's laboratory.

Marvin ignores me as I wander around his lab and look at the experiments he has set up. On one table, he has a beaker of something dark pink—like beet juice—on the boil over a Bunsen burner. On another, he has several sticks of explosives standing at attention like soldiers. On another, he has a frog, ventral side up, and a set of dissection tools.

"Do you want to cut it open?" he asks, turning in his swivel chair.

"I want to ask you questions," I say.

"Okay."

"Do you think my guilt organ is plausible?" I ask.

"Maybe," he says. "I will go looking for it the next time I have a specimen." I nod at this even though I know this means he will cut open one of his friends.

I ask, "Why do you think humans are so—"

"Dumb?" he interrupts.

"I wasn't going to say that," I say. I was going to ask why humans are so guilty all the time. But since he said this, I add, "Not all humans are dumb."

"Most of them are. You know that. Why else did you come here?" he asks.

"I don't think most humans are dumb," I argue.

"So you think most humans are smart?"

"I think all humans have potential."

He seems disappointed.

"I was going to ask why humans are so guilty," I say.

"They're guilty because they're dumb."

"Humans are not dumb," I say again.

"Stop saying that!"

I shake my head and go back to walking around his laboratory. I try to think up something to say so I seem normal—just like Gustav told me to be—but I can't think of anything.

"HUMANS ARE NOT SMART. YOU KNOW THIS!" Marvin yells.

I sigh. "I think a lot of humans are lazy, yes. I think we could do better as a species. But I don't think I'm smarter than humans. I *am* human, am I not?"

"You're a human with an IQ of one hundred and seventy-five."

"It's just a number," I say.

"You shrug? You're given this gift and you pretend you

don't have it? You think numbers mean nothing? You're no scientist. Get out of my lab."

"It's an equation. Mental age divided by chronological age times one hundred," I say.

"YES!"

"And how does this explain that you think humans are dumb and I don't?"

"You're young. You don't know anything yet."

I don't say aloud that nearly every study ever done on IQ shows that IQ decreases with age. I don't say anything except "You're right." I say it not because he's right. I say it because Gustav told me to act normal.

I reach up to the area where my theoretical guilt-free gland is.

Marvin laughs and says, "That's more like it!"

He tells me he's putting a control group together this week. He tells me he thinks it's real. A real undiscovered gland that can solve many world problems. I don't see a spark of understanding in his eyes when he says this ironic thing.

I don't mention that if the solution for many of the world's problems is here, then no one else will ever be able to solve their problems. Only the seventeen people who live here.

China Knowles—Friday Afternoon—Broadway

I am China, a girl sitting upside down on a bench in Central Park. Every ten minutes I sit right side up so all my blood doesn't pour out of my nose or my eyes. That's what it feels like upside down. It feels peaceful and I can't hear the ticking, but it also feels like my head will explode with blood.

It's getting late.

It's getting so late that I realize I don't have a plan.

My plan was: Leave home, find Shane, make new plan, execute new plan.

My plan now seems to be: Sit upside down on a park bench until I can figure out what my next plan is. The sky is cloudy, but it doesn't feel like it will rain the way the man on the bus said it would.

Shane hasn't called back. My mom hasn't even called back. I tried to call Stanzi at around three but there was no ringing, just the sound of distant helicopters with rotors made out of cotton balls. Her voice mail is gone.

I'm hungry because there's a praline vendor nearby who is candying nuts and it smells good. Maybe pralines will make me vomit again. Maybe this is a side effect of turning right side out. Maybe I'm doomed to vomit everything now that my digestive system is on the inside.

I try Shane again. No answer. No voice mail to talk to. Just ringing to infinity.

I decide to buy pralines. I buy three bags of them and they are too sweet but I eat them anyway as I walk down Broadway toward the subway station.

But I pass the subway station and keep walking down Broadway because maybe I'll run into Shane. Maybe he's taking a walk to clear his head. Maybe he got a job at the pizza place near 54th Street where he took me on our first date. Maybe he's a bicycle courier. Maybe he's a businessman. Maybe he's a skyscraper. Maybe he's the *W* on top of the Westin hotel.

As I walk, I get closer to Times Square and the tourists are out. Country people from another state and another time. People who speak French. Schoolchildren in matching purple T-shirts with chaperones who don't hear the ticking coming from every trash can on every street corner.

If I'm close to Times Square, then I'm close to Port Authority.

Your Runaway Plan Has More Self-Esteem
Than You Do

I am thinking now
of buying a ticket
and sleeping in my
own bed by myself
and being right side out
and being happy.
I am thinking now of
the stuffed monkey ashes
in the back porch fire pit
and thinking
maybe I was too rash
maybe I was too quick
maybe I was too trusting
maybe I was stupid
to think
that anyone wanted
me any more than I
wanted
the monkey.

I walk to the doors of Port Authority and a homeless man asks me for money, so I give him a five-dollar bill. I call my mother, but the ringing blends right into our voice mail message, which is my sisters singing some dumb song from the Disney Channel show they watch all the time.

I miss them.

I'm a failure.

I buy a ticket home.

I walk down the steps to the gates.

I'm underground. I feel the weight of all of New York City on my chest.

And then I see Shane.

He's not here to find me.

He's here to leave...with some guy who is old enough to be his father.

He doesn't see me. But he will.

Patricia—Friday Morning— Act Normal

IN THE PLACE OF ARRIVALS

We're leaving today. I am mourning the loss of my pianos. I am mourning the loss of my manuscripts. I try to act normal around Gary, so when he asks if I'm off my period and we can make love, I say, "Maybe tomorrow."

When he takes his loud morning shit, I gag.

When he says, "I think I was wrong about your weird music. You should be open to experiment here. Think outside the box. That's the point, I guess." I smile and act like he said something that pleased me.

On our walk to lunch, he says, "Why do you think those two came? They don't belong here. This generation is lost."

"People said that about our generation, too," I say.

"This is different."

"I don't think it is," I say. "I think the real world changed.

I don't think we're the right people to debrief anyone who comes from it." I add, "I think they'll fit in fine here."

"Marvin says the girl has potential, but she's some sort of humanist."

"Nothing wrong with that."

"I don't know," he says.

I don't think I ever heard Gary say *I don't know* before.

"You're not yourself." I put my arm around his shoulder and he wraps his around my waist and to any onlooker we would look like friends or lovers when, really, I am a genius about to escape from a genius prison.

Lunch is uneventful. Gary has been east because I told him that was where I found Stanzi and Gustav. He didn't even get a half mile into the forest, but he says there's no sign of anyone walking out there. So now he's planned a search involving all of us. Every direction. All day. All weekend if we have to, until we find the helicopter and destroy it. He doesn't tell them about the destruction part, though.

He asks Gustav, "Do you think you can remember which way you walked into camp? Or which way Patricia brought you?"

Gustav says, "I'm pretty sure I know where we came in. I can show you."

I discover Gary looking at me and I smile because I know I won't see him tomorrow. I think of Kenneth and I smile even wider. I say to the new arrivals, "Before we go, let me show you the garden!"

On cue, the three of us stand up and put our plates and utensils in the sink.

In the garden I talk to Stanzi silently, in her head.

Me: *We're leaving today.*

I know.

Me: *I can't thank you enough for rescuing me. I owe you my life.*

She thinks, *We're rescuing you?*

Stanzi—Friday Afternoon—
The Dinner Bell

IN THE PLACE OF ARRIVALS

After an afternoon walking in circles around the south perimeter of the forest, Gustav looks exhausted. I want to tell him to sleep. I want to tell him he shouldn't fly while exhausted.

"Do you think you can see the helicopter today?" he asks.
"It's not Tuesday."

"I trust you," I answer.

"That's not what I asked."

I fiddle with my hands. My nails grow faster here. Or maybe I didn't trim them before I left. I think about what day it is. It's Friday. We arrived yesterday morning. We will leave as the geniuses eat dinner. As I rip my index fingernail shorter, I feel sad for Gustav. "You worked so hard," I say. "It took you months."

"Why are you sad?" he asks.

I shrug. "Because it didn't work out," I say. I don't want to use the word *failure*, so I think this is a good compromise.

"It's working out," he says. "It's all working out."

I look at him, but he looks over my shoulder and I turn around to find Gary approaching from behind me. He tells Gustav that the recovery mission will move west next, toward the old west field—which is our field—and I stand there thinking about if Gary will miss Patricia when she leaves with us today. I don't think he will.

Then a voice inside my head starts talking to me.

It's her.

The other me.

She is panicking. She says, *What are you doing? How can you take off with so much extra weight? Why aren't you staying? Why did you leave? What if you crash? What if when you come back the school really blows up? What if when you come back the tests all come back as zeroes? What if when you come back, Gustav doesn't love you? What if when you come back, no one likes you anymore? What if they think your lab coat is weird? What if they think you should do more to your hair? What if you're not Stanzi? What if you're not Stanzi? What if you're not Stanzi?*

Stanzi—Friday
Afternoon—430

IN THE PLACE OF ARRIVALS

When we're alone, I say, "I don't understand why we came at all. Why did we come?"

"We came to get Patricia."

"I didn't know this," I say.

"Neither did I," Gustav says. He looks at his watch, then whispers, "It's four thirty now. Do you want to go check if you can see the helicopter?"

"No."

"Why not?"

"I don't care if I can see it. I trust you."

I'm about to whisper to him about fuel, but he says in my head, *The fuel is in the tank. Patricia took care of it. We're ready to go. I just have to get some things in the house.*

I whisper, "But we can't take anything with us. The load will be too heavy."

He smiles. "I only need the map. I don't care about anything else."

"I have the map," I say. "The bush man told me to keep it safe, so I stored it in my underwear all this time." I pat my backside.

●○○○○

Patricia meets us in the house. She looks nervous. She's wearing a thin dress with short sleeves and has goose bumps on her arms. She says to me, inside my head, *Do you have the map?* I nod. Gustav notes that we are communicating and looks dejected.

Patricia says, "Don't worry, Gustav. We won't talk about you behind your back." At this, Gustav excuses himself to go to the bathroom.

She says in my head, *He loves you. Have you talked about that?*

I think, *Not really. It's been a strange day.*

She thinks, *It will all work out once we're home.*

I think, *I want to see Marvin one more time. I want to bring his cures home with us.*

That's not allowed, she thinks.

But it's not fair, I answer.

"What's fair?" she says.

Gustav flushes the toilet. Patricia says, inside my head, *Gustav knows the plan. Just follow him when the dinner bell rings.* I reach up and massage my guilt gland the way Marvin told me to, but it's not guilt I feel, it's anxiety. We all know this escape is dodgy. I sit down at the kitchen table and write

a poem for China, so she might understand everything when
I get home.

How to Tell If Your Alternate Universe Is Real

If you have kept a scratchy, dog-eared map
in your underpants for thirty-two hours.
If you have whispered so much that you can
hear other people's thoughts in your own head
and you don't think that makes you crazy
then your alternate universe is probably real.

If you have lost your faith in humanity by
looking at the people who consider themselves
better than humanity. If that makes you
want to throw up and scream out
This is the nature of human suffering!
Then your alternate universe is most likely real.

If you hunger for another trip
to an empty school, no matter if it means
another drill, a thousand ovals, no
matter if it means you will be in infinite danger,
then your alternate universe is unquestionably real.

○○●○○

The dinner bell rings.
    Patricia heads to the dining hall looking peaked and I

realize that she will probably play her Lansdale Cruise cramps card again. We pretend to follow for a minute, and then we turn back and head up the long, steep path to the field where the helicopter is. I try not to be nervous. Every time my other me, the one who thinks I'm not Stanzi, talks in my head, I tell her to shut up.

She says, *You are not who you think you are! You are not as strong as you think you are! You can't go on like this forever— wishing and hoping and pretending that frogs are important. Gustav is not a frog.*

She says, as I jog through the thorny underbrush, *I never had control over your nose or your hands. I never had control over anything. Stanzi has control. And you are not Stanzi. You are _____. You must realize this or the helicopter will never fly.*

"Shut up!" I yell. Gustav either doesn't hear me or doesn't care. Maybe he has a voice in his head, too. Maybe his voice tells him he is not Gustav. Maybe his voice tells him I love him. I hope so.

When we arrive at the field, I can't see the helicopter.

I feel awful about it. My other says, *You can't see anything because you are not Stanzi.*

Gustav gets into the cockpit and starts the motor and the rotor begins to revolve and the sound is there—a gentle *thwap-thwap-thwap*. I panic. Who else can hear it? Who else will come? Will they shoot us as we take off?

I say, "Can I help?"

He says, "We have to empty everything from the back so

Patricia can fit." We throw our things onto the field and when I stop and look at my dissection kit, Gustav looks sad for me. He produces a scale and asks me to step on it. In my jeans, shirt, shoes, and lab coat, I weigh 145 pounds. He weighs himself. In his jeans, shirt, and shoes, he weighs 155 pounds. He says, "You have to take off your shoes."

When he says this, he strips down to his boxer shorts. There are tiny pictures of trucks on them. I don't comment on this.

He weighs himself again. 149.

I take off my sweatshirt as well as my shoes. 140.

"What's our maximum weight?" I ask. "Can we make it?"

"Patricia is forty-three years old," he says. "My guess is that she is ten pounds heavier than she looks. Probably a hundred and fifty."

"She's only five foot five!"

"Trust me."

"So? Will it fly?"

"Four thirty."

"What?" I ask.

"Four thirty. That's the maximum weight."

Patricia appears at the edge of the clearing. She is only in her near-transparent dress. Now I understand why she was dressed so poorly for the weather. She's as light as she can be.

But when she weighs herself, she is 149.

We are eight pounds overweight.

I remove my lab coat and take off my jeans, shirt,

underwear, and bra while Gustav looks over the map and removes a small piece of the helicopter's body. I replace my lab coat. 138.

Patricia removes her dress and sandals. 146.

Three pounds. We are three pounds short.

Gustav tells us to get into the helicopter. Patricia curls up in back where our box of things once was and she shivers in her small pair of underwear. Gustav also looks cold. I will not remove my lab coat.

Gustav puts his headpiece on and tries to take off, but the helicopter will not fly.

Patricia says, "Hurry up! They're coming! They know!"

Gustav tries again and the helicopter lifts slightly off the ground, but we set down again with a small thud. He looks at me. Then he takes off his boxer shorts and Patricia takes off her panties and I'm the only person not naked in our helicopter and I can hear Patricia inside my head saying *Take off your coat! Take off your coat!* And I can hear the other me saying *You are not Stanzi! You are not Stanzi!*

Gustav has already thrown my headset out onto the grass. He tries to lift off again and I can hear the motor trying, but he will not push it.

I hear him thinking.

Stanzi, you have to take off your coat.

Don't worry.

We will all be naked.

But this is the only way out.

"Hurry!" Patricia yells again.

I jump out of the helicopter and take off my lab coat and leave it in the field. Gustav helps me back into the passenger's seat and presses the lift lever and we rise. And we rise. And we rise.

Only five minutes after our escape do I hear Patricia crying.

I ask, "Why are you crying?"

She says, "Because we're all naked as babies."

Gustav says, "We're babies being born."

I say, "I have some things I need to talk about."

China Knowles—Friday Evening—Tommy

I am China—the girl you saw passed out and naked on Facebook. I stand three gates away staring at Shane, but he is turned into the man's chest. Not too close, but close enough. They're at gate #26 waiting to board a bus to New Jersey.

I walk toward him and say, "Shane?"

He looks up and his eyes are the color of saffron. He is a lizard. His long, sticky tongue snaps out and says, "Who are you?"

The man seems amused. He is wearing a suit that cost a lot of money. I don't understand why he is taking a NJ Transit bus and not a limousine in that suit.

I stare into Shane's reptile eyes.

Nowhere in them do I see recognition. He doesn't know who I am even though we're soul mates. He's become something else now. In a short week, he has turned himself inside out and we can see his lizard.

"Sorry," I say. "I thought you were my friend Shane."

"His name isn't Shane," the man in the nice suit says.

Shane stares.

I hold up my bus ticket. I say, "Shane?"

"You have the wrong boy," the man says.

You have the wrong boy.

I back away from them both. Shane is a lizard. I'm a digestive system. One of us is right side in and the other one is right side out. The man is grinning about something and I don't know what it is. He seems to not know Shane. This isn't his father or his caseworker or his uncle or . . .

There is a gate call for their bus.

My bus doesn't leave for another fifteen minutes.

I stand frozen, Shane's yellow eyes blinking vertically at me, blinking in code.

He doesn't want to go to New Jersey with this man. That's what the code says. The man met him on the Internet. On the site where we met—our safe place.

I swallow myself right there in the lower level of Port Authority.

It's a taste like nothing else. It hits all the taste buds. Bitter. Sour. Sweet. Salty.

I'm a pulsating stomach staring at a lizard boy.

This is when he recognizes me. His lizard eyes blink more code.

Help me. That's what he says. He says, *Help me.*

He has a small suitcase at his feet. Not his. It's expensive and it has wheels. As he and the man in the suit start to move forward with their tickets, I follow them and Shane keeps eye contact as he panics, his vertical lids snapping open and closed so much I can't keep up with what he's saying. *Help me. Help me. Help me.*

As the man in the suit takes care that his luggage is stored under the bus in the right bin, I move.

I grab Shane by the arm and we run back into Port Authority. I don't look back and I head for the stairs. We hear the man yelling "Tommy! Tommy!" behind us.

My Screen Name Has More Self-Esteem Than I Do

I chose Olivia
not for any reason
except that it was
late at night and
I wanted to feel normal.

You chose Tommy
because you said it
sounded masculine
and childish
at the same time.

○○●○○

We can hear him from where we are huddled in the handicapped stall in the Port Authority women's bathroom.

"Tommy! Tommy!" the suit man yells. He says something about how the bus is waiting. Something else about taking back all the things he'd given him. Something else about the night before.

At that, Shane starts to cry. He's sitting on the toilet and I'm standing by the door in case anyone trusts the man in the suit more than us.

They always do.

They always trust the man in the suit.

Shane's head is in his hands and his tears start to drip down onto the old red tile. The man in the suit asks a woman to check the stalls for him. The woman says, "Get out of the women's bathroom!"

I want to call security. I want to call 911. I want to call anyone, but there's no one to call. Just like last time. No one to call. So I rub Shane's scaly lizard back and tell him it's okay. And he rubs my duodenum and tells me it's okay.

And we sit there for an hour.

When we leave, he's afraid the man will be waiting for him. I tell him we should turn right side out again and he tries, but can't do it, so I stay digestive and buy two new tickets back to Pennsylvania.

Next bus is in ten minutes.

"Why did you come?" Shane asks me.

"I was going home. I gave up. You never answered my calls. I figured...you know."

"I'm a lizard," Shane says.

"Don't worry," I say. "I'm a stomach."

"I'm damaged," he says.

"Not beyond repair."

"I'm not sure," he answers.

"Trust me," I say.

We walk toward the stairs back down to the gates, each of us looking for the man in the suit.

"He's not here," I say.

Shane says, "He probably wants his money back."

I don't ask Shane what the man in the suit paid him for. I know enough about Shane to guess.

"I'd like to hear him argue that in a court," I say.

"Where will we go?" Shane asks.

"I'm taking you home."

He sighs. "I've never lasted at home. Not mine. Not anybody's."

"Then you tell me and we'll leave the minute you can't last anymore."

We get into line for the bus and Shane turns toward the wall. The line starts to move. We get onto the bus. I have my backpack. Shane only has his phone and the clothes he's wearing.

"Can we go shopping when we get there? I need some clothes."

"Sure. Until then, I'll borrow some clothing from Gustav. You'll like him."

"Is he damaged?"

I say, "We're all damaged."

"Oh."

I say, "You'll fit in nicely."

Stanzi—Friday Evening—
Twenty Questions

We are flying through blue skies and there is nothing I can see but my naked body because I cannot look up.

There is a scar on my right leg. It's fourteen inches long and nearly an inch wide. It's dark, like the color of my deepest gums.

I stare at it.

○●○○○

If I said, "When I look at the scar, it all comes back to me," then I would be lying.

It never went away, so it can't come back.

Not for any of us.

○○○○●

Gustav is first to speak. We are half an hour away from the Place of Arrivals. We are departing. The map clearly indicates that THERE ARE NO DEPARTURES. I don't know how to read a helicopter map, but if I did, I would be able to tell you that Gustav is not following the same route as when we arrived.

Gustav says, "I'm sorry it's so cold."

Patricia says, "It's not your fault it's cold."

Gustav says, "I think I meant I'm sorry we're naked."

"Naked isn't bad," Patricia says. "We're like babies."

"I guess it could be symbolic," Gustav says.

I can feel them both waiting for me to talk, but I'm looking at my scar. It's easy to avoid when showering. If I don't look down, then it's not there.

"I don't think birth is this cold," I say.

"True," Gustav says.

"I don't even think death is this cold," I say. "My sister was six years old. Last time I held her, she was warm."

No one says anything.

I say, "Right before then, we were playing Twenty Questions. It was my turn. I was eight. I chose *wombat* because I knew she didn't know what a wombat was."

No one says anything.

It's just me and my scar.

My scar has a mouth.

It says, "I just kept saying *It was wombat! It was wombat!* as we lay in the back of the mangled car waiting for someone to help us. Wombat. I don't think I've said *wombat* since that day. Not one time. Not even in biology. Wombat."

I slap it. I slap the scar for saying it. I slap the scar for saying anything.

246

"Stanzi?" Patricia says. "Stanzi?"

"I am not Stanzi. I am _____. I have always been _____."

I slap my scar again. It doesn't feel anything. My legs are numb from the atmosphere. I'm numb from the atmosphere. I have always been numb from the atmosphere.

The scar speaks through my slapping. "I watched as she tried to breathe. I felt her die. She had peanut butter and jelly saltine crackers stuck to her arm. They were her favorite. She never knew what a wombat was and I was trying to trick her because she was so impatient all the time. Six-year-olds are supposed to be that way, though. That's what Mama and Pop always told me."

"Oh, Stanzi," Gustav says.

"Wombat wombat wombat. We used to play with my microscope together," I say. "We used to play State Tag—a game we made up to remember the states. She always pronounced *Tennessee* wrong."

"Oh, Stanzi," Patricia says.

"I never let her cross the road by herself. I never let her eat too much candy. I muted the commercials on children's TV so she wouldn't get brainwashed. I told her nobody could ever actually look like Barbie. I told her she was smart all the time. I taught her how to make her own cheese sandwich once.

"But she still didn't ever know what a wombat was and it was an unfair advantage."

Gustav leans into me and gives me a half-hug. I feel Patricia's cold hand on my shoulder.

"I wanted to be Stanzi forever," I say, inspecting the red slap marks around my scar. "I just wanted to be Stanzi and you could be Wolfgang and everything would work out okay. I thought we would stay there. I thought it would be good for us. I thought we could be free."

Stanzi—Saturday Morning—
Family Vacations

It's impossible to sleep naked in an invisible helicopter. It's possible to fake it, but impossible to actually do it.

Patricia sang through the night. She wrote a song about being free right there, curled into a ball on the floor of a home-made helicopter in the middle of the night. She has a beautiful singing voice.

Gustav looks twice as tired as he did yesterday. He's shivering.

"I can sit near you or something. Keep our body heat up."

"You can't move. We're balanced."

At this, Patricia laughs.

"It won't be long now," Gustav says.

"It won't be long until what?" I ask.

"Landing."

"But it took us nearly two and a half days to get there."

"The journey back is half as long," he says. "Isn't that what you always say about the vacations you take with your parents?"

I look down at my scar again.

It opens its mouth before I can put my hand over it. It says, "I don't go on vacations. I lied to you."

"Where do you go?"

In my head, I explain everything to Gustav and Patricia. Out loud, I say, "I write you postcards, but I never send them."

"But you said you lied. I don't understand. How would you get postcards if you're not on vacation?"

My scar talks. It tells them everything about my family vacations. Everything. Where we go. Why we go. How the world is falling to pieces.

I ask Patricia if she's still happy to come back with us. "You were in a safer place," I say.

"Safety is a lie. It's a ham sandwich without the ham," she answers.

"It's a blue sky on Monday when it rains on Wednesday," I say.

She says, "I'm so sorry about your sister."

○○●○○

I daydream with my eyes closed. There are four coffins. Mine is red, Mama's is blue, Pop's is green. The fourth coffin is half the size of ours. It has a unicorn painted on it, and a rainbow. Mama and Pop are lying with their eyes closed, but every few seconds they peek out to see if I'm sleeping yet. So I pretend to sleep, and when they are convinced, they get up, join hands, and head to a big coffin that is propped in the corner. When they open the door of the big coffin, I can hear the sound of people laughing and talking and clinking glasses. Only when they close the door behind them do I squint and see that the big coffin is Chick's Bar.

And it's just us here now. Me in my red coffin and her in her unicorn coffin.

There are wombats everywhere.

Lansdale Cruise—Saturday Morning—No Kidding

Last night, I talked to the bush man. He told me he knew about what happened with the newsman. "Things go around," he said.

"No kidding," I said.

He said Stanzi and Gustav will come home. He said they're bringing him a woman. He said the woman wrote a song last night about being free. He told me her name is Patricia. I asked him if we could stop sending the bomb threats now.

"It's hard to stop a machine once it's in motion," he said.

"It's like the answers," I said. "I think you gave us the wrong answers."

"It's hard to stop a machine once it's in motion," he said again.

"Whatever," I said.

"Whatever?"

"Whatever. I want to stop lying now. Right now. That's why I came to see you."

"I will miss your hair," he said.

"You have bags of my hair. Let's trim this into something cute. Like a bob or something."

"Would you like me to put a bowl on your head and cut around it?"

"You're a sculptor," I said. "I want you to use your imagination."

I walked out of the bush with my hair sculpted into this woman, Patricia. From every angle there was another Patricia. Her face, her hips, her breasts, her eyes. My head was a hundred Patricias. I was a walking museum.

He gave me a lowercase *e* that was beaded with pearls. He told me that I have to do the interviews now because the man and cameraman went back to LA.

When I got home I washed my hair and then I went on the Internet to find a style I liked and I watched a how-to-cut-your-own-hair video and gave myself a decent layered bob.

OOO●O

Today is different. When my dad asks me what I did last night, I tell him, "I went and saw the man in the bush. He sculpted my hair into a hundred statues."

He doesn't even look up from his paper.

"You should at least look up to see my hair," I say.

He folds a corner of the paper down and squints at me.

"Looks nice," he says. "A little short, maybe, but hair grows back."

Every Mrs. Cruise so far has had hair down to her ass. Always blond, like mine. Always highlighted and no roots showing.

"I don't think it's too short," I say.

"A man in a bush?" he asks.

"I'm thinking of getting it cut shorter, actually."

"It's *your* hair," he says.

I turn on the kitchen TV and scroll through the channels looking for a cooking show and stop when I see the newsman's face. The minute I see it I want to start lying again. I turn the volume up so I can hear him.

He's talking about whales. He's talking about how whale-watching tourism is booming again in California. At the end of his report, a helicopter flies overhead and he says something unintelligible and points at it. Then he apologizes to the anchorman and says it's an inside joke between him and his cameraman.

"I had sex with that guy two nights ago," I say.

My dad folds down the corner of the paper again and slides his glasses from his head to his nose. "Him?"

"Yeah," I say. "Total poseur."

"Looks it."

"He's from Ohio but tells everyone he's from California."

He says, "Isn't that the channel with the annoying weatherman?"

China Knowles—Saturday Afternoon— The Monkey

I am China, girl who swallowed herself yesterday in Port Authority, New York City. I'm China, girl who unswallowed herself this morning in my kitchen, right in front of my parents. My little sisters are staying with my aunt. Shane is still asleep on the floor of my room.

"Mom told me you burned the monkey," Dad says.

"Yeah. Sorry about that."

"I know I never see you anymore," he says.

"Yeah. I know you have to work," I say. "I'm really sorry about the monkey. I really liked it. I'm glad you bought it for me."

"I wish I could be here more often," he says. "I really should be in your life more."

"It's fine. Mom has us covered."

I look at Mom. She wears a look of worry.

I'm China with a boyfriend sleeping in her room and no

one knows that but me. Mom and Dad seem to think I ran away from home because of the monkey.

○●○○○

I call Lansdale because she'll know what to do. Lansdale knows exactly how to use a fire extinguisher without having to stop and read the instructions.

"Is this China?" She answers her phone like this, as if I've been gone for a month.

"Yes."

"I think the answers were wrong," she says.

I tell her that the answers don't matter. "Shane is here. Still asleep in my room. My parents are home."

"There were sixteen leftover answers," Lansdale says. "Sixteen!"

"What do I do?" I ask.

"Don't take any more tests with those answers," she says.

"I'm talking about Shane."

"Oh," she says. "Just keep him in your room. Close the door."

"What if he has to pee?"

"Can't he pee out a window or something?"

○○○●○

I'm China and I'm on my bedroom floor with Shane, who is crying. My parents are downstairs making a late lunch and they dance to Cuban music in the kitchen. They can't hear me when I tell Shane to stay in my room. They don't hear me as I tell him to pee out the window.

He isn't a lizard anymore. We talked about that.

The world will be upside down forever. We have to come to terms with this.

Shane has to smoke. He says he can do that out the window, too. My phone rings and it's Lansdale.

"Is that guy actually pissing out your window?"

I look over at Shane, who is pissing out the window. "Yes."

"The whole neighborhood can see him," she says. "A side window would have been a better choice."

"Oh. Well."

"I saw Kenneth last night," she says.

"Is that the guy from Los Angeles?"

"The man in the bush," she says. "He gave me the wrong answers."

"Oh," I say.

"He said Stanzi and Gustav are coming home."

"His name is Kenneth?"

"Yes."

"Why didn't anyone tell me that?"

"I thought you knew," she says. "Is he smoking out the window now? Seriously. Someone's going to call your mom and tell on you."

I ask Shane to move. While I close the front window, I stop and wave to Lansdale three doors down across the street. She's perched on the front porch with two quiches cooling on the windowsill.

257

"Cute apron," I say.

Lansdale says, "Kenneth also told me we could stop now."

I say, "Fuenteovejuna?"

"Yeah. We had the wrong answers. It doesn't matter anymore."

"Shane wants to meet my parents," I say.

"Let him."

"But."

"What have you got to lose?" she asks. "Let him. But make him chew a breath mint first. And wash his hands. Smoke never makes a good first impression."

Stanzi—Saturday Afternoon— Gustav's Secret

This is where we land and I'm home, right? This is where my bed is, yes? My books? My other coat? My other lab coat?

I wake up to the gentle whooshing of the rotor and we are still naked ice-cube babies in the sky. When I look forward, I picture the windscreen and the control panel, which Gustav is using every so often, pressing buttons and moving levers. But I can't really see anything. It's Saturday.

Ten minutes ago, I thought I hallucinated the whole helicopter. I could see the red. I could see the propellers above our head.

But now, nothing.

Just the three of us floating through the air in impossible positions. Patricia is still rolled up like an injured pill bug. Gustav is sitting upright with nothing on except his headset. He's still shivering.

I say, "I just had a dream about four coffins. You weren't in any of them."

"That's nice," Gustav says. He actually means it. I think he's relieved to not be in my coffin dream.

I go quiet.

I look back at my scar. It stays quiet.

"I have to tell you something," Gustav says.

I nod.

"It's something important," he says.

"Okay."

"I have two letters from the bush man. I got them about five months ago."

"And?"

Gustav looks flustered. "And you know how I got them."

"Yes."

"So?"

"So," I say. "So what?"

"You know what I did?"

"I think so."

"I kissed him," he says.

"What letters did he give you?"

"Does it matter?" Gustav asks.

"Yes."

"A blue *B* and a black *G*. Both carved from wood."

"I wonder what we could spell with all of our letters," I say.

"Are you listening?" Gustav yells. "Are you listening to anything?"

"I don't care who you've kissed before me. I only care who you kiss after."

"But he's a guy. What if? I mean, what if?"

"I love you," I say. "I really don't care if you love me back."

"I do love you back. I've loved you since ninth grade in the cafeteria when you pulled out your dissection kit to eat lunch."

I look down at my scar, which is still not speaking.

I stay quiet for five minutes. I know it's five minutes because I count. Have you ever counted five minutes? It's long when you count it. There have been 375,840 five-minutes since ninth grade in the cafeteria when I ate my faux chicken nuggets with my scalpel and my forceps.

"It was a pickup truck," I say.

"It ran a stop sign and Pop didn't see it," I say.

"I only saw it when I looked over to tell her that my Twenty Questions answer started with a *W*," I say. "I saw it coming straight for us."

"What was her name?" Patricia asks from her pill bug position in the back.

"Yeah," Gustav says.

"Her name?" I ask.

I look back at the scar.

Stanzi—Saturday Afternoon— Her Name

I can't remember her name. I can't remember it. I knew it yesterday. I knew it every day since she was born warm. But right now, naked in the sky, I can't remember her name.

Gustav says we'll land in five minutes and neither he nor Patricia seems particularly bothered that I can't remember my own sister's name. Unlike all five minutes that came before it, this one is unfathomably short. I can see our oval-shaped neighborhood. The tops of the fifteen-year-old trees. The playground. The parallel road. Las Hermanas. Gustav's backyard. And in the distance, I can see my house, brown siding and bilevel.

We descend.

We descend.

We descend.

And the bush man runs toward us. And Gustav's father

opens the garage door. And his mother holds a tray of home-baked cookies. And suddenly I remember that we're all naked.

And I can't remember her name.

The scar can't remember her name.

No one remembers her name.

She was the kid who didn't know what a wombat was. She was exceptional at geography. She liked rhyming. She talked too loud. She had temper tantrums when she had to go to bed. She will never kiss the bush man. She will never go to a dance. She will never watch *M*A*S*H* with me while we eat frozen dinners. I will never tell her that Hawkeye Pierce is our mother. She will never cry out my name at night and set up her sleeping bag on my bedroom floor.

We land and the grass doesn't know her name. The dirt. The dandelion blooms. None of them know her name.

I don't know what comes after this.

I don't know what comes after this.

Reset. Reset. Reset.

The Interviews IV—
Saturday

Lansdale Cruise finds her camera, sets it to video, and stuffs it into the pocket of her apron. She rushes to the scene in Gustav's yard with a quiche in each hand.

When she arrives, she sees that they are naked—Gustav, who is covering his privates with a tea towel; an older woman, who is wrapped in the green plastic tarp that Gustav's father uses to cover his woodpile during the winter; and Stanzi, who is covered in blankets and is sitting on the grass, staring toward the backyard.

Interview #1 Patricia

Lansdale asks, "Why are you all naked?"

"Are you filming me?"

Lansdale makes her camera nod and says, "Yes."

The dangerous bush man pushes Lansdale away and says, "Not now."

Interview #2 The dangerous bush man

"Why did you give us the wrong answers?"

"Turn off the camera," he says.

She turns it off. The bush man walks away from Patricia, who is getting partially dressed in Gustav's mother's clothing. The tray of chocolate chip cookies lies, unscathed, on the macadam outside the garage door.

"How do you know they're the wrong answers?" he asks.

"Because there were sixteen extra."

"And?"

"And sixteen extra means you got us the wrong answers."

"Or you remembered them wrong," he adds. "You've been distracted, haven't you?"

"I guess."

"Test week wasn't ideal," he says.

"No."

"So what were you asking me?"

"Nothing, I guess," she says.

Interview #3 Gustav

"Why are you all naked?"

"We had to make weight," Gustav answers.

"What's up with Stanzi?" she asks.

"I think she's in shock. Or something. I don't know."

"Did you call her parents?"

"My dad did. Their message says *Gone to bed. TV dinner in freezer. Make sure you turn out the lights.*"

"They're at Chick's Bar," Lansdale says.

"Oh," Gustav says. "I'd better go tell my dad."

Interview #4 Stanzi

"Stanzi?

"Stanzi?"

Lansdale stares at Stanzi. She waves her hand slowly in front of Stanzi's face but Stanzi continues to stare forward with glassy eyes. Lansdale puts her video camera on the grass and starts taking Stanzi's vital signs.

"Stanzi!"

Stanzi doesn't answer. Her eyes are fixed. Her breathing is shallow.

Lansdale walks back to the group standing around the open garage door.

"She's in a stupor of some kind," she says.

○○○○●

Lansdale produces her two quiches.

"Kenneth said you were coming back today. I figured you might be hungry." She hands Gustav's to him now that he is fully dressed in a tracksuit. She puts Stanzi's in her blanket-covered lap and Stanzi doesn't move. The quiche falls into the dip in her crisscrossed legs. Lansdale leans down to balance the aluminum foil pie dish on Stanzi's lap, but it won't balance. She opts for leaving it in the grass in front of Stanzi.

266

Lansdale walks back to the bush man and tells him, "I'm not cut out to be an interviewer."

"You're not great."

"You set me up to fail."

"I guess."

"That's why you gave me the wrong answers," she says.

"If you say so," he says.

China Knowles—
Early Saturday Evening—
My Type

I'm China, the former rectal canal, and I'm going to introduce Shane to my parents.

Dad left for a business trip without saying good-bye, but he left me a card. It's one of those sappy cards that are made from textured paper and use script font. There's something on the front that's trying to impersonate a poem, but it's so thick with adjectives under the *I Love You Daughter* title that I can't read it.

Inside, Dad wrote *You're always my little girl.*

Considering I'm about to produce a boyfriend from my room, I'm glad Dad isn't here, especially because he thinks I'm still his little girl.

Mom should be okay with this.

Why wouldn't a woman who walks around in latex and who washes her sex toys in the dishwasher want to work this out? She has to have a solution. Shane has told me it's okay to use his background as a way to soften her up.

"I want you to meet somebody," I say.

"That's the same thing you said when you won that awful goldfish from the Boy Scout stand at the block party."

"This time, he's a little bigger than a goldfish," I say.

Shane walks in and sits on the couch next to me.

"Mom, this is Shane. Shane, this is my mom."

"Hi," Shane says.

Mom smiles. "It's about time. That dumbass Irenic kid wasn't your type."

"Wasn't my type?"

"A mother can tell these things," she says. "Plus you look a lot healthier now, after this running-away drama. Did you go vegetarian or something? Your skin looks fantastic." Then she turns to Shane. "Where do you go to school?"

"Uh. Nowhere at the moment," he says. "I—uh—I just moved."

"Oh. That's nice. How'd you two meet?"

We both stutter a bit, and then say it simultaneously. "On the Internet."

"You were Internet dating?" she asks me.

"Not quite," I answer.

Shane laughs.

"Anyway, I have a big favor to ask," I say. "It's, like, a huge favor."

"A huge favor," Shane repeats.

"Can Shane live here for a while?" I ask. "I mean, just until we can find him another place to live or something?"

Mom tilts her head.

Shane says, "I ran away from my foster home last month.

And then I was staying in New York with some other friends from our group."

"Your Internet group?" Mom asks.

"Yeah. But then it got annoying hanging out with people in real life."

"It got annoying hanging out with people in real life?" Mom repeats.

"Yeah."

"Well, how does China know she won't be the next person you leave because you don't like hanging out in real life?"

This is a good question and I'm happy she asks it.

He says, "I love China. I know what she's been through. She knows what I've been through. We understand each other."

"Was this one of those game chat rooms?" Mom asks. "I hear about those."

"It doesn't really matter where we met," I say. "Shane needs a place to stay."

"I'm not a foster home. You're not eighteen. I don't know if you're running away from people who're looking for you. This is no small favor."

"It's a big favor," Shane says. "But I promise you, no one's looking for me. I'm free of the system. I could go back for help, but foster homes aren't really helpful. I mean, for me. I'm sure they are for other people, I guess."

She looks at me. "So you went to New York to bring him back?"

"I went to New York so I could stay there. But it turned out this way by accident."

"You weren't going to come back?" Mom asks.

"No."

"What about your sisters?" she asks.

"What about them?"

"They would have been devastated. And me. And Dad."

"I'm sorry," I say. "There are things you don't know."

"There are things I don't know?"

"There are things you don't know," I say. And then I hear a familiar sound. *Thwap-thwap-thwap.*

Mom goes into the kitchen and returns with a piece of paper and a pen.

"Write on that paper what I don't know." She puts the paper on the coffee table and goes back to the kitchen. She says, "Shane, what do you like to eat? I was going to make dinner tonight for myself and China, but I think we should celebrate by ordering Chinese or pizza or something."

I whisper to Shane, "She says this almost every night."

"I'd love a pizza," Shane says.

"Pizza it is," Mom says, then disappears into the down-stairs bathroom.

And it's me and a piece of paper and a pen and Shane and the truth and I'm fighting every urge I have to swallow myself. *Thwap-thwap-thwap.*

Stanzi—Early Saturday Evening— Talk to the Screen

I'm a television in your living room. I'm watching from inside.

You carried me from the helicopter to the grass. You crossed my legs so I could balance. You wrapped me in blankets.

You put a quiche on my lap but it wouldn't balance. You took my pulse. You checked my pupils. You moved my arms and let them flop down to my sides.

You kept calling me Stanzi. *Stanzi Stanzi Stanzi.* And you know it's not my name, but you called me Stanzi anyway and then you called the doctor and she came with her medics and you put me in an ambulance. You found my parents. You sobered them up with black coffee. You told me I would be okay, but you don't know what's wrong.

I don't know what's wrong.

Ask my DNA. Ask my little chimera. Ask your television what it wants for dinner and it won't answer back.

I have a dream. There are no coffins. There are no wombats. There is a blue sky. There are two clouds. I'm on one cloud. You're on the other. You're a thousand people. I'm one. You're one person and I'm two. When you ask me questions, I understand them, but what do the answers matter?

China Knowles—
Early Saturday Evening—Hospital

There are sirens. This can't be good.

I call Lansdale while Shane sits at the table with the pen and paper, offering to tell my mom for me, and I tell him no.

"Stanzi is in a stupor," Lansdale tells me. "They took her to the hospital."

"She's in a stupor?" I say.

"Yes."

"Is Gustav okay?"

"Yes. He's at Las Hermanas with Kenneth and a woman named Patricia. He said he wanted tamales," she says. "Has Shane met your parents yet?"

"Yes," I say. "Stanzi's in the hospital?"

"Yes."

"I think we should go see her," I say, and hang up.

I take the piece of paper and the pen and I write *Mom, Stanzi is in the hospital and we've gone to see her. I'll talk to you later about what you don't know. I did go vegetarian, though. Thanks for noticing.*

Stanzi—Saturday Night— Dr. *M*A*S*H*

China is right side out, unswallowed. She brought Shane. I know this because she comes right up to my face and yells as if I can't hear her through my human screen. She says, "THIS IS SHANE!"

But I'm a television with no remote control and I can't say anything or do anything except think on the inside. I can think on the inside. I think, *I am eighty-nine cents' worth of chemicals walking around lonely.*

Lansdale is pacing. Her hair is shorter and it maintains its structure when she talks to China or Shane. Mama and Pop have gone home. They didn't leave a note for me because they know the nurses will feed me and turn out the lights.

I don't have any homework, but I wish I did.

I wish I had a worm to dissect. Or a bird. Or a frog. Maybe if I had something to do with my hands, I would do it. I've tried reaching for my guilt gland a hundred times since we landed, but I can't move my arm.

I can only blink.

I think I'm drooling.

China looks worried.

She holds a poem up to my face, and I see it as a block of text, but can't read it because my eyes can't move.

The doctors asked Mama and Pop if they knew what was bothering me. I watched as Mama put her hand on Pop's lap and told them about the years of therapy. The PTSD. My nightmares. My obsession with biology.

Obsession. They called it an obsession.

The doctor asked if we were in family therapy. Mama and Pop said, "We're fine." I'm inside this television, looking out. Even I could tell the doctor didn't believe them. And if she had half an olfactory system, she'd have smelled the gin two doors away.

Another doctor comes in and asks China, Shane, and Lansdale to leave.

He sits on my bedside and says this:

"_____, you're a one hundred percent healthy girl with a bright future. I understand you had something traumatic happen to you when you were eight years old, and I'd like to talk about it."

I'm inside the television looking out. He's a funny man, this doctor. He looks like Sidney, the psychiatrist from *M*A*S*H*. I'm Hawkeye Pierce. It's the final episode of *M*A*S*H* and I know it by heart. We're fighting over what happened in the back of the bus. Sidney knows I'm lying when I tell him that the lady in the back of the bus smothered a chicken. He knows she smothered her own baby. He knows I'm damaged. He knows I will never be the same again. He knows I'm split in two, no DNA test needed, no need for tetragametic chimeras, no need for biology.

All I need is my lab coat. I have two more of them. They're in my bedroom closet.

China Knowles—Saturday Night—
House of Letters

I'm China and I am no longer a walking anything other than a human being.

Lansdale and Shane and I go to talk to the dangerous bush man.

He's not in his bush so we ring the doorbell at his house.

When he answers the door, he's dressed in shorts and an old T-shirt with the sleeves cut off and he's not wearing his trench coat. He invites us in, but we stand at his doorway looking in.

Patricia sits, freshly showered and hand-combing the knots from her hair. She is naked, but not in a bad way. In front of her is a lamp that shines hot light onto her and in front of the bush man there is a block of plaster already partially carved, white dust on the floor, of her basic shape.

"Forgive me," the bush man says. "I can't stop working."

He leaves the door open and we stand on the doorstep and watch him pare away at the block of plaster in long, sweet strokes.

"If you come in, please try to be quiet," he says. "My mother is sleeping upstairs."

We can't come in. It's too full of quality letters. There's a kitchen and each plate is a letter. Each fork. Each glass is a letter. Every inch of the walls is a letter. Every crack in the ceiling, every spill on the carpet. Every piece of furniture is a letter. Patricia is sitting on an *L*. The bush man is sitting on an *M*. The door is an enormous lowercase *i*.

We can't walk through the *i*.

"My house is full of answers," the bush man says.

This is when we realize we don't understand the questions.

○●○○○

I'm China, girl with many questions, girl with no answers.

Shane asks, "What's with that guy's house?"

"The dangerous bush man loves letters," I say. "It's his thing."

"Oh."

Lansdale says, "Doesn't really clear anything up, does it?"

"No," Shane answers.

"You'll understand," Lansdale says. "Our town is very strange."

"Our town is very ordinary," I say.

"What will you do about your friend?" Shane asks.

"Stanzi will come back," I say. "She probably needs more therapy."

"Her lab coat," Lansdale says. "She needs her lab coat."

"Yes," I answer. "Let's take it to her."

When we get to Gustav's house, I ask him if he'll come with us and if he'll bring *Amadeus* with him.

We are a gang of four teenagers now. We walk down the street as if we own it because we do own it. It's our street. We were born here. We'll either stay or we'll leave depending on how you treat us.

Stanzi—Sunday Morning— Mental Health Profile

Last night they shoved me into a giant doughnut called a CAT scanner and took some other tests. I heard them all talking. The EKG tech was nice and actually talked to me. The chest X-ray people talked about a concert they wanted to go to—as if I was a cat on the dissection table. As if I was a frog. At least the nurse who catheterized me was nice.

Then I was officially admitted. They dressed me in paper clothing. They called this a *voluntary admission*. I can't volunteer for anything. I'm a paper doll who pees into a plastic bag. I'm a Mental Health Profile with a needle that feeds saline into my blood. Saline. Seawater. Tears. No one here knows they are filling me with helicopter fuel.

○○○○●

Gustav, China, Lansdale, and Shane are hiding under my bed right now. The nurse is here to check my IV and the first doctor of the day is the psychiatrist who looks like Sidney from *M*A*S*H*.

He says my parents will be here soon and I'll get my own room after that.

"Would you mind asking your friends to leave?"

I'm inside a television. I can't tell my friends anything. All I can do is drool.

"That's a cool coat. You trying to fit in around here?" he asks.

I try to move my arm to feel the sleeve of my lab coat, but I can't move anything. I'm inside a television and it's all clear now. Gustav was wrong about everything. There are no insects. My dreams were wrong. I know how to waltz.

We are babies being born.

I can't feel my lab coat, but I know China and Lansdale dressed me—flopped me forward to get it over my back, lifted each arm and slid them into the sleeves, smoothed it out under my butt. They knew not to button it. They knew to put a pen in the chest pocket, but pens aren't allowed here, so they pretended.

"We'll see you later," China says to my television screen.

"I'll bring you a cake," Lansdale says.

"Get better," Gustav says.

Shane doesn't say anything. He's cute. You can see his damage all the way down to his toes. China will never save him completely. That's what my television brain says. It says: *China will never save that boy.*

283

Mama and Pop are here. They tell the doctor I was fine all this time. They tell him about my good grades and my group of friends. They tell him about how we spend a lot of time together.

"We go on vacations several times a year," Pop says. "Once we went to Scotland."

The doctor looks at me. "That sounds nice," he says.

"We went to Colorado twice last year," Mama adds.

The doctor looks at Mama. "That does sound nice. However, I think the problem here is not lack of vacation time. There's something deeper."

"Ask her if she misses her cat," Mama says. "She raised it since it was a kitten."

Inside my television head, I'm laughing. I laugh so hard, I think I accidentally spit a little and a snot bubble forms at my nose. Mama, Pop, and the doctor look at me then, waiting for a breakthrough. As if the breakthrough is inside me, not them.

The doctor tells them this is a matter of *flipping the switch* inside my brain. I want to ask *Which switch? There are more switches in here than there are on Gustav's cockpit control panel.*

"I want to recommend family counseling," the doctor says. This is the third time he's said it in twenty-four hours. Pop hangs his head. Mama follows suit.

If I could speak, I'd say: *Gone to bed. TV dinner in freezer. Make sure you turn out the lights.*

They move me to a room that has a plastic window. Mama and Pop have told me this is the psychiatric ward.

I am in the looney tunes.

Mama looks mortified that of my friends, I landed here first. She says it right in front of me, as if I really am a television. "What about her friend who built the helicopter no one could see? Why isn't he in here?"

Pop says, "It's not his turn. It's _____'s turn."

"This isn't a game," Mama answers.

"I didn't say it was," he says.

She walks up to my screen and yells at it. "This isn't a game!"

They both keep looking at their watches. They must have somewhere to go. Anywhere but the looney tunes. When they finally leave, I'm alone in my room.

I say, "Her name was Ruth.

"I called her Ruthie.

"Sometimes I called her Ruthless if she was on my nerves.

"I taught her how to braid yarn. I taught her how to pull a splinter from her own finger. I taught her about the antibiotic properties of dog spit. She taught me everything. She taught me everything about life and how to have real fun."

China Knowles—Sunday Morning—
Little Shit

I am China, and I'm sitting with my mother at the kitchen table. Shane is playing video games with my sisters upstairs.

Mom has a piece of paper and a pen in front of her.

She slides them to me.

"I'd rather just tell you," I say.

"Then tell me."

All that comes to me are poems about weathermen.

"Or write it down," she says. "Your choice."

"Your weatherman has more self-esteem than I do," I say.

"Okay."

"How to tell if your snowstorm was real," I say.

"Okay."

"Did you notice that I swallowed myself?" I ask.

Mom shifts in her seat. "It was hard not to notice."

"Why didn't you ask me back then?"

"Because stomachs can't talk," she says.

"I don't want to call the police," I say. "I don't want anyone to know."

"That's not up to you and you know it," she says. She is stiff in her seat now. The mention of police. The look on my face. "If this is about that asshole in the bush, then someone has to do *something*."

"He's a good guy," I say.

"Kenneth? Shit. He's a psycho."

"He's a sculptor. He's eccentric. That's all."

"I have letters," Mom says. "I know about Kenneth."

"It's not about Kenneth," I say.

She pushes the paper toward me. She knows I communicate best on paper. Upstairs, there is loud yelling and laughter. Upstairs, my sisters are playing a game and they're happy, like I want to be.

I write and talk at the same time. I write: *Last summer I was dating Irenic Brown.* I say, "The night before he broke up with me, he raped me." I write: *I didn't know what to do, so I didn't do anything.* I say, "He told me that no one would believe me anyway."

Mom sits there looking at me. I'm not crying or even emotional. I'm like Stanzi—talking about biological facts. I'm like Gustav, building machines that can take us to invisible places. Mom finally says, "Irenic Brown?"

"Yes."

"That little shit."

"Yes."

"That little piece-of-shit asshole."

"Yes," I say.

"What a little shit piece-of-shit asshole!" she says. She has angry tears. She is pacing now. She says, "He told you no one would believe you?"

"Yes."

"I believe you," she says.

"There's more," I say.

"Oh." She sits down again.

"He bragged about it on Facebook. He took pictures."

She stares at her hands and clenches her jaw. I know she wants to ask how many people saw it or how many people know or how many people could sit in a witness stand and say something about it. She says, "What a slimy piece-of-shit asshole."

"Yes."

"Oh, China," she says. "You need help. You can't do this alone. I don't know what to do to make you feel better. I don't know anything about this. I don't even know who to call."

"I've called them already."

"Who?"

"Everyone I could call. Crisis lines, mostly."

She moves her chair next to me. She sits and holds my hand.

I say, "Then I found this place online for victims. I met Shane."

"Oh," she says. And I see her compute that she has left her young daughters alone with him upstairs. And then I see her compute that she shouldn't be computing that.

"He's been through worse."

"It's different for everyone," she says. "Not better or worse."

"He's been through worse," I say again. "Trust me."

"I know who you can talk to," she says. "Katie. From my group. She's—uh—she's had experience with this."

"Your group?"

"My friends," she says. "You know."

"Your basement friends?" I ask.

"Yes."

"I don't know if that's a good idea."

"Probably not."

"Yeah."

"I'm going to get you into therapy," she says. "I'll ask Katie who I can trust."

"Okay," I say.

"We should call the police," she says.

"Not now."

"We should. It was only last summer. Other people…" She stammers on the *N* sound of *know*. "Know. Other people know."

"Not now," I say again.

"Shane can stay with us," she says.

"Thanks."

"I'm so sorry this happened. I don't want to ask details, honey. I don't. But I'm your mother. I have to ask some things."

I want to ask her to write them down on the piece of paper, but I don't want to answer any questions. What happened to me is something everybody knows and no one knows. It's something everybody cares about but nobody cares about. It's as common as cereal for breakfast. There are laws that say it's illegal, but barely anyone goes to jail for it.

I say, "I have to go back and see Stanzi. Before you ask me anything, call the crisis center. The people there are nice. Or call your friend. Talk to her. Just let me go see Stanzi first."

"Okay," she says. "Can I hug you?"

"Sure."

"Do you mind if I cry?" she asks, but she's already crying. It doesn't seem possible that I made the neighborhood dominatrix cry, but maybe it was about time she paid attention.

China Knowles—Sunday Afternoon—The Gland

I'm China and I'm at the hospital and they are searching through my purse. This morning I had to beg to take Stanzi her lab coat, and they let me because Lansdale said it would help her.

I let them keep my whole purse at the security desk. I don't need it.

I walk down the hall to Stanzi's room and hope I'll be the only one there.

And I am.

Her eyes are closed and she seems to be sleeping, so I sit down in the chair that's nailed to the floor next to her bed.

"I'm sorry I never talked to you about it," Stanzi says. It startles me.

"You're awake."

"Did you hear me? You were in pain. You were wronged.

I should have talked to you about it. I should have helped you in ways friends help each other."

"You did," I say.

"I ignored it. You turned into a stomach. You wrote so many poems."

"You did what you could," I say.

"I'm sorry."

"You really shouldn't be."

"I'm sorry for a lot of things," she says. "I'm sorry for everything."

She's looking right at me and she's not drooling anymore. Her arms are crossed over her chest and her lab coat is buttoned.

"They nearly didn't let me bring that in this morning," I say. "Said you could eat the buttons."

"Why would I eat the buttons?"

"You're in the psych ward. I guess they think you could do anything."

"Last week, I flew in an invisible helicopter to a place that doesn't exist," she says. "How do I explain that to these people? How do I explain that I'm not the problem?"

"You might want to leave out the helicopter part," I say.

"If I leave it out, then Marvin is right and the world is dumb."

"Then you'll be in here for a lot longer and people will think you're nuts," I say. I have no idea who Marvin is, but I don't care.

"Not when I show them the helicopter."

"Stanzi."

"I *am* nuts," she says.

"You aren't nuts."

"I have post-traumatic stress disorder."

"Yes."

"I'm obsessed with biology because I don't know how to have fun. I'm obsessed with biology because I want to cure something I can't cure."

"What's that?"

"Guilt," she says. "I think I nearly have it figured out. Touch here," she says as she touches a part low down on her neck. "Lower. Yes. Just there. That's how to cure it. That gland right there."

I am China, the girl who was once a weathergirl. I'm sitting in a hospital chair and my friend Stanzi is telling me how to cure guilt. As I massage this part of my neck, I feel better. I think Stanzi is a genius, but everyone else here will think she's crazy. I don't know how to tell her this.

"It's okay," she says. "I already know."

"What?"

"That everyone here will think I'm crazy," she says. "Don't worry. I'm not really going to tell them about the helicopter. Or the cure for guilt."

I wonder if I just said that out loud.

"No," she says. "You didn't."

○○○●○

Mom and Shane have had a discussion.

When I walk in, they're sitting at the kitchen table and my

sisters are sitting in front of the TV in the den watching the Disney Channel.

I turn off the TV and tell Shane and Mom to join us in the den and I sit upside down on the couch. Little sisters do what big sisters do, so they do it, too. Shane has a look of concern on his face for me, but I smile and say, "Come on. Do it."

Mom is the last to turn upside down, but once she does, she giggles a little.

"The world is upside down," I say.

"It is," Shane says.

"I think my head is going to blow up," my sister says.

"It won't blow up," I say. "Stanzi told me heads don't blow up. She's a biology genius."

"It really feels like it will," she answers.

"Look at how different everything looks now," I say.

"I'm dizzy," Mom says. "How long do we have to do this?"

"I don't know," I say.

○○○○●

Once the girls are in bed, Mom, Shane, and I gather around the coffee table in the den and talk about how we'll make this work.

Shane says, "I'll go to school with you now."

I say, "I'll show you the best places to go during the drills."

"Shane will have a room in the basement," Mom says. "I talked to your father and he thinks that's the best way."

I ask, "Shane's going to sleep in the dungeon?"

Shane looks concerned.

"I'll redecorate it tomorrow. You'd be surprised what I can do in a school day," she says.

"Stanzi talked today. She told me she won't be back to school for a week or two. They'll let her out soon, but she has to do group therapy or something. She seemed okay," I say. "I'm glad she talked."

"That's good," Mom says.

"Yeah," Shane says.

"I think we should go to the police," Mom says.

Shane stays quiet.

"The police won't believe me any more than they can see Gustav's helicopter."

"Irenic Brown has a reputation," Mom says.

"And so do I," I say.

The three of us look at each other around the table.

"Shane showed me your website—the place where you met," Mom says. "I can't make sense of what I can do to help. I feel so guilty."

I reach over and I put Mom's hand on her neck in just the right spot. I tell her to rub it. "That should help," I say.

"I called a crisis center," she says. "I was going to call Katie about her therapist, but I couldn't bring myself to tell her." She looks despondent. "You're my daughter," she says. "This is a nightmare."

Stanzi—Monday Two Weeks Later—
Project Evidence

Gustav built a helicopter in his garage and no one believed it.

But today, he's going to fly it to school and show them. I'll be on the bench in front of the WELCOME sign, sitting upside down like China does. I'll be wearing my lab coat because no one in my group therapy thinks it's weird and they tell me *Whatever works.*

Thwap-thwap-thwap.

As I walk toward Gustav's house, I see that the bush man Kenneth has decorated his entire yard with sculptures. They are nudes of Patricia. There are forty of them, at least. I see him and Patricia sitting behind the bush having tea and they wave me over.

"We've thanked Gustav, but couldn't thank you," they say.

"You don't need to thank me," I say.

"Yes. Yes, we do."

"I didn't know anything. I didn't know where we were going. I didn't know we were coming back. I didn't even know that you weren't a dangerous man," I say, looking at Kenneth. "And I didn't even know you existed," I say to Patricia.

"You saved my life," Patricia says.

"I don't think I did," I say.

Thwap-thwap-thwap.

I didn't tell my group about the invisible helicopter because it's sacred. It's something I didn't want to talk about. When the question came about my "disappearance" with Gustav the week before, I told them they were outrageous and that I hadn't disappeared at all. I told them Gustav loves me and I love Gustav.

I told Mama and Pop, too, and Mama said we are all headed for the looney tunes. When she said that, I asked her what was so wrong with the looney tunes.

She answered, "I don't know." She answered, "People talk."

"What about the master list?" I asked. "It's like going to the looney tunes over and over again. What good does it do?"

"It does us good," Mama said.

"It shows us that we're not alone," Pop added.

I told them Dr. Sidney-from-*M*A*S*H* wants to do family therapy. They told me they are looking forward to it. We'll start next week. I'll start by telling them that visiting those places makes me feel more alone, not less alone. I'll tell them I don't want to go anymore. I'll show the doctor my snow globe collection. He'll probably recommend that I throw it away.

And then I'll tell them about Ruth and how she didn't know what a wombat was and I'll massage my neck and maybe, just maybe, it will work.

○○●○○

When Gustav flies to school and lands the helicopter in the football field, several students point to it. It's Monday, so I can't see it. But they can. One of them is a girl from my bio lab and I wonder if she'll be the woman Gustav marries.

China and Lansdale see me on the bench and they sit down on either side of me. They do not sit upside down like I sit. Lansdale has a pixie haircut. It's new and cute and none of us talk about it.

"I think Gustav should love a woman who can see his helicopter every day," I say. "Don't you think that would be fairer?"

"Fairer to whom?" China asks.

"To Gustav."

Lansdale says, "I read a lot about this stuff. Nowhere does it say that a wife must see her husband's helicopter every day of the week."

"You *are* the expert," I say.

"Plus, love doesn't just show up and disappear. Not real love," she says. "I've known enough Mrs. Cruises to know that some people just show up and don't have any love at all. They just have needs."

"Irenic Brown," China says.

"Yeah," I say.

"No. I mean Irenic Brown," she says. "He's coming over here."

I stay in my position with my hair dangling in the grass beneath the bench. China tenses. Lansdale runs her hand through her hair and says, "I'll take care of this."

Irenic stands there staring at Stanzi. "It's good to see you back, Stanzi," he says. "We were worried about you."

"You're a piece of shit, you know that?" Lansdale says.

China stays quiet. She doesn't look like she'll swallow herself from down here.

Lansdale continues. "You're a piece of shit who doesn't understand anything. You think you're so powerful now? We talk, you know."

"We take screenshots, too," I say, upside down.

them in a file.
We take screenshots of every girl you brag and we keep

"You don't have to be so mean about it," he says.

"The guilt will eat you," China says.

"You will suffer for the rest of your life," I say.

"If some daughter's father doesn't kill you first," Lansdale says.

Irenic Brown walks away.

Maybe he didn't know until now that he was feeling guilty. Maybe he didn't know that he should.

When first bell rings, there is no announcement about a drill. The police car is not stationed outside. Mr. Man-with-a-Gun's parking space is empty.

○●○○○

I get to be Mr. Bio's helper all day. My obsession with biology is something I'm supposed to work on, except I can't go into the back lab without staring at the animals in the formaldehyde jars.

Mr. Bio discovers this and takes me to another small lab. He shows me a box.

"I have a project for you," he says. "If you want it."

"Okay," I say.

He opens the box. It is full of Ziploc bags. Each bag contains an item and has a pink note stapled to the outside.

"What is this?" I ask.

"Evidence."

"Evidence of what?"

"That's the question, isn't it?" he says.

He hands me a box of latex gloves and a clipboard with sheets of paper clipped in. I'm still looking into the box. I see a Baggie with something familiar in it.

It's a frog liver, a hex nut from a helicopter kit, and a lock of blond hair.

Gustav sent me a postcard at lunch. It said: *We are not eighty-nine cents' worth of chemicals walking around lonely. Love, Gustav.*

China and Shane sat together at a table with me, Lansdale, and Gustav.

There are no bomb threats yet today.

●○○○○

I have cataloged four pages' worth of Ziploc bags. Mr. Bio says the buses are here. I don't want to leave. I'm finding the answer. I'm working hard.

He tells me, "You have all week. This is your special project."

I look at him as if to ask, *Why?*

"The principal said you were the one who should do it."

"She thinks I'm guilty," I say.

"She thinks it's a mystery," he corrects. "She thinks you're the one who will solve it."

"But there was no drill," I say.

"We haven't had one in a week," Mr. Bio says. "Or maybe two weeks." He scratches his chin. "Funny how you forget, isn't it?"

"What about makeup tests? Don't I have makeup tests?"

"We haven't had one of those in a week or two, either."

"How will they assess us without tests?"

"I don't know. Maybe this is your test." He gestures toward the box of evidence.

I look at my list of cataloged items. Frog livers, hex nuts, red food coloring, a condom, a baseball, a tube of lipstick, a clarinet reed, a tiny pair of Barbie boots, a dried flower, a war medal, a coupon for dog food, a tiny ship in a tiny bottle, a sock, a pin for an air pump, a pill bug, a compact of eye shadow, a protractor, a fork, a razor blade, a cigarette, a pocket Latin dictionary, a Led Zeppelin cassette tape, toothpaste, an arrowhead, a necklace with a panda bear pendant, a pacifier, hand sanitizer, a scrap of paper with the anarchy symbol on it, a nail clipper, a cello bridge, a dried-out bull's eyeball, a miniature Slinky.

I look back into the huge box and I put gloves on and root through the other items on the surface. I see something shimmering halfway down. A small letter *S* covered in silver glitter.

I meet China and Lansdale on the bus. Gustav is still on the football field with his physics teacher, who will agree to give him credit for the helicopter if ever she can see it.

As the bus takes off, I can see Gustav in the pilot's seat. Because it's Monday, I can't see the helicopter, so it just appears as if Gustav is floating, in the sitting position, in front of Ms. Physics. If that wouldn't make you believe, what would?

China Knowles—Monday Night—
They All Do

I'm China and I'm a walking iambic pentameter after reading sonnets for an hour at the end of the school day. Shane sits
with a new friend on the bus—a kid he met in his government
class. He looks happy. No one knows he's a lizard inside. No
one knows he's mine.

We decided to keep that a secret.

My mother logged on to our survivor site last night and has
asked the collective what she should do to help me. I haven't
looked at the answers, but she texted me twice today to tell me
she loves me and I didn't find it too intrusive.

We can't figure out if we should tell Dad when he gets
back or not.

I told her I didn't want him looking at me any differently.

"He won't," she said.

"They all do," I said.

We decided to talk about it again another time.

Lansdale, Stanzi, and I sit in my basement, now half Shane's room and half not-Shane's-room. I tell them I have no poems today.

"You always have poems," Lansdale says.

"And you always have long hair," I say.

"This is all my fault," Stanzi says.

I say, "Okay. I have one poem." I hand it to Stanzi to read it, but I realize that she's weaker than I am now, so I take it back and I read it myself.

How to Tell If Your Life Is Real

If you wake up and you
no longer own a stuffed monkey
and you no longer own
a sweater that shames you
and you no longer fear
anything because someone
said
I
believe
you
then your life is probably real.
If you go to bed and you
no longer fear waking up
and you no longer fear
a boy who shamed you

and you no longer fear
telling the truth because
someone said
I
love
you
then your life is undeniably real.

When I'm done reading the poem, we decide to go see the bush man, Kenneth. As we approach his corner, we hear music.

Then, before we can see who's playing, he grabs me and takes me into the bush by myself. He hands me three poems. My poems. I don't know where he got them. He says, "These are good. These are the answers."

Stanzi—Tuesday Morning— I Crawl Through It

Today is Tuesday and I can see Gustav's helicopter parked on the football field. I skip homeroom and go to him.

Yesterday we visited Kenneth and Patricia in the bush. We told them how we feel about each other.

Gustav said, "We've decided to fall in love."

I said, "My doctor recommends against it, but sometimes doctors are wrong."

Gustav is on the football field with his physics teacher, who still cannot see the helicopter.

"It looks brand-new," I say.

Gustav says, "I waxed it."

"It's beautiful," I say.

Ms. Physics seems curious enough. She seems open-minded. She *wants* to see the helicopter. She looks at me and says, "Point to the tail."

I point to the tail.

She says, "Point to the altimeter."

I step up into the cockpit and I look at all the dials. I know it's the one marked *ALT*, but in case I'm wrong, I ask Gustav, "It's the one marked *A-L-T*, right?"

"Yes."

I point to it.

Ms. Physics says, "Where is the pitch lever?"

I shrug. "I'm not a pilot."

Gustav climbs in the passenger's side and points to the pitch lever. "Here is the pitch lever and here is the engine oil gauge and I removed part of the horizontal stabilizer in order to make weight on my last flight."

We are two high school seniors floating in front of a physics teacher.

And still, she cannot believe.

○○○○●

As I walk the hallway with my late pass, I walk past open classroom doors. In one room, they are having a mock trial. In another, they are filling test tubes with suspicious liquids. In another, they are having a race on the blackboard. In another, they are writing a play for kids in middle school. The play is about being a good sport.

When I reach the biology room and weave my way past the dead formaldehyde frogs, I find my box full of evidence. It has been sealed with sturdy packing tape. My clipboard is gone.

I look for Mr. Bio but he's not here. His briefcase isn't next to his desk. His lab coat is hung on a hook by the door.

It's just me and the frogs.

I pretend that one of the frogs is Mama.

I pretend that another one is Pop.

We have a conversation about Ruthie, my dead sister. We have a conversation about how she didn't know what a wombat was. I tell them I was a bad big sister.

Mama weeps, mostly.

Pop tells me I was a great big sister. "Remember how you taught her how to braid Mama's hair?"

I open a drawer in the lab to find a tissue for Mama-frog. Her tears will overflow the formaldehyde jar soon. When I open the drawer I find the tests. Just the answer sheets. Thousands of little dots. Tens of thousands of letters.

I'm on my knees by the drawer. I take out stacks and stacks of answers and place them on the floor. The drawer is ten feet deep. It's ten feet wide. I empty it. I'm cold and sweating. In the very back of the drawer, there is a hole.

I crawl through it.

I fall through a chute of some sort.

"YOU HAVE BEEN ASSESSED!" the principal says as I land in her chair, in her office, on her lap.

We are surrounded by heaps of paperwork. She's eating peanut butter crackers and asks me, "Don't tell anyone, okay? I'm not allowed to have peanuts."

"Okay." I shift on her lap to make us more comfortable.

"How did you get here?" she asks. "From the parking lot?"

I point up. "Biology lab. A drawer."

"Oh, that."

"I was supposed to be cataloging evidence."

"Investigation is over," she says. "We found our man."

"Man?"

"Yes," she says, picking up the crumbs of her crackers by touching each one with a spit-soaked finger. "He's out on the lawn for public display."

○○○●○

On the front lawn of the high school, there are a hundred students in a circle. It reminds me of the drills, but there are no drills.

In the center of the circle is Kenneth, the dangerous bush man.

The students throw things at him. Countries and capitals, history, dates, names, triangles, circles, rectangles, infinitives, clauses, equations, couplets, limericks, theories, debate points. Someone throws hydrogen. Someone throws radium. Another throws xenon. I see Lansdale Cruise in the crowd.

"Why are we doing this?" I ask her.

"He can take it," she says.

"Everyone here is guilty," I say.

"Everyone here knows it," she answers.

China arrives. She's holding a piece of paper that says *Irenic Brown*. She throws it at him. The crowd stops hurling shapes and phonetic symbols and x and y. Kenneth, the dangerous bush man, says he knows what to do with Irenic Brown.

"I know what to do," he says. "Only no one will let me do it."

China looks as if she knows what this means.

When I listen to the crowd thinking, I hear they know what it means, too. I consult myself: *Do I know what this means?*

I think it means we must start paying attention.

I know the odds of this happening are very low.

Stanzi—Monday Afternoon—Frogs in Jars

There is a note on the table. It says *Gone to bed. TV dinner in freezer. Make sure you turn out the lights.*

It's only four o'clock.

So I walk over to Chick's Bar and find them at the corner table. When they see me, they climb underneath and hide. They climb into two jars of formaldehyde and become frogs. I pick up the jars and take them home.

○○○○●

The doctor from my family therapy arrives. He still looks like Sidney from *M*A*S*H* and I know he can save the frogs that are now sitting on the breakfast bar.

We sit in a circle. Me, Mama-in-a-jar, Dr. *M*A*S*H*, and Pop-in-a-jar.

I say, "They're dead frogs floating in formaldehyde."

"I'm sitting right here," Mama says. "I *am not* a dead frog."

Pop doesn't say anything.

"Why do you say this, _____?" the doctor asks.

"Stanzi," I correct. "My name is Stanzi."

"Well then, Stanzi, why do you say your parents are dead frogs? They're sitting right here."

"They won't talk about Ruthie," I say. "And they take me to school shooting sites and call it vacation."

Dr. *M*A*S*H* looks at Mama and Pop for verification. They nod but don't seem to see that their vacations are in any way creepy.

"I talk about Ruthie all the time," Mama says. "I never stop talking about Ruthie."

"I have never heard you talk about Ruthie," I say.

"That's because you weren't listening," Pop says. "We talk about her all the time."

"Is this true?" Dr. *M*A*S*H* asks me.

"No."

He looks at me like I'm an insect, lying to make my life harder.

I say, "They drink all day at Chick's Bar. They drink all night, too. They leave me a note that says *Gone to bed. TV dinner in freezer. Make sure you turn out the lights* every night."

"Is this true?" he asks them.

"We've never left a note like that in our lives," they answer.

I walk to the sideboard and open the middle cabinet door and remove hundreds and hundreds of notes. They all say *Gone to bed. TV dinner in freezer. Make sure you turn out the lights.* Some are on white paper. Some are on the backs of junk mail. Some are on sticky notes. I pull them all out and place them, in piles, on the kitchen table.

"Is this your handwriting?" the doctor asks them.

"Yes," Mama says.

"Do you think Stanzi wrote these herself?" he asks.

"No," Pop says.

"And do you talk about Ruth, the way you said you did a minute ago?"

"No," Mama says. "If I had to talk about it, I would end up in the looney tunes."

"She would," Pop agrees.

I'm still on my knees clearing out the sideboard of notes.

There is a hole in the back of the cabinet.

I crawl through it.

○○●○○

I'm in the dangerous bush man's bush.

He is here, naked and drinking tea with Patricia.

I say, "Why did we go all that way only to come back?"

"You know why," Patricia says.

"Because you're in love and needed rescuing?" I ask.

"I didn't need rescuing," she says. "I was on my way here anyway. Eventually."

The bush man says, "I could have taken Gustav's helicopter and gone myself."

"But you didn't."

"No."

"You made us go," I say.

"I didn't make you do anything," he says, then offers me a madeleine cookie.

"Love is funny, isn't it?" Patricia asks.

Thwap-thwap-thwap.

I sit and chew my madeleine cookie and I wonder if I could be Constanze Mozart and if Gustav could be Wolfgang and if we might, one day, sit naked in a bush drinking tea. This morning we kissed on the grass in his backyard. There is a lovely evergreen behind the birdbath.

"I think that's possible," Patricia says.

"Anything is possible," the bush man says.

I ask for another cookie for Gustav, who is landing the invisible helicopter where we kissed earlier this morning, and they give me three. I leave the bush and walk across the street to see him landing right where we landed two weeks ago. Back then, I was a naked frozen baby being born. This time I'm Stanzi, wearing my lab coat, crawling through holes.

Gustav jumps out of the invisible cockpit and I walk over to him and give him the cookies.

He says, "She gave me credit."

"Did she see it?" I ask.

"No."

"But she gave you credit?"

"Full credit."

Today it's a red helicopter. Who knows what people will believe tomorrow?

Stanzi Has a Paper Clip

Gustav is building a boat. I can see it every day except on Thursday because that's family therapy night. When I talk to Gustav about the boat, he doesn't tell me it will be better than a stupid human. He tells me it cannot drive itself.

○●○○○

Gustav's boat is red, just like his helicopter. He's decided that he wants to be in my coffin dreams again and asks if he can have the biggest coffin. I tell him yes, but I don't tell him that in my coffin dreams since we flew back, I dream us in a double coffin. I make a note to change it to queen-sized so we both have more room.

Mama and Pop now make dinner together and last night they made *carnitas* and they were delicious. Gustav ate with us, and Pop and he get along great. Mama avoids Chick's Bar because once she came out of her formaldehyde, she said she never wanted to smell like that again.

We threw away the master list. It's in a landfill now. Probably the one over by the highway. You're welcome to it if you want to one day see the looney tunes.

●○○○○

There are still intruder drills once a month. Red buttons. Test weeks. Banned books. Dress codes. Assessment. Detention. We can't get away from it. Letters make letters make letters make letters. It's a chain of command. A line of duty, a battle chosen.

Gustav has chosen the battle of building an invisible red boat. I have chosen the battle of remembering what I wanted to forget. Lansdale has chosen the battle of being an honest, short-haired girl. China has chosen the battle of being right side out.

We're alive. We have words and shapes and ideas. We will throw them at you when you do not believe. We will throw our love and our hate and our failure and success. We'll split in two right in front of you and be our best and our worst. We'll lie and tell the truth.

But we are alive.

And no one has the answers.

And we all sent the bomb threats.

We did it so you would believe.

318

Because we believe.

We believe.

Somewhere in every mind is an opening to crawl through.

Somewhere in every body there are eighty-nine cents' worth of chemicals walking around lonely.

And somewhere in every idea there is a hole that fits an unbent paper clip.

You just have to find it.

Reset. Reset. Reset.

Acknowledgments

I am Amy, the walking circulatory system. I bleed, I pump, I recycle. Yesterday I was inside out and wrote a book. Today I am right side in and I am grateful.

The usual suspects deserve enormous thanks. Michael Bourret, you told me you liked weird. Look what happened. Andrea Spooner, please edit this sentence so it somehow conveys the full appreciation I have for your trust. Deirdre Jones, you rock all over. All other LBYR teammates, thank you for everything you do for me.

I am also grateful to the community at Vermont College of Fine Arts for responding so positively to a reading on a humid summer night in 2013. Thank you.

Family and friends, you know who you are—thank you. Special thanks to e.E. Charlton-Trujillo, mi hermana en Las Hermanas; Wendy Xu, for your illustrations in this book and for your amazing *Angry Girl Comics*; Robyn Sarig for your hospital expertise; my kids, who make my world surreal and who don't fit into ovals; and Topher, because you built me an invisible helicopter.

Teachers, professors, librarians, and booksellers: You are my heroes. I want you to take one minute now and smile about the important work you do. You are loved. I thank you for reading my books, for sharing them with your friends and colleagues, and for sharing them with your students and patrons.

Student readers, thank you for reading. Thank you for writing to me. Thank you for being you. You are not ovals. You are not letters. You are human beings, and every time someone rolls their eyes at you because they think your opinion doesn't count, picture me giving them the finger.

Questions for Discussion

1. The novel's narrators are all burdened by unacknowledged trauma. How do they each attempt to cope with it? Why are their initial methods unsuccessful?

2. How do the characters' surreal descriptions of dealing with pain—for example, Stanzi splitting herself, and China turning herself inside out—hint at the root of their trauma?

3. Kenneth, the bush man, appears throughout the novel as an alternately menacing and understanding character. He sells letters for kisses but also offers cryptic advice. What do you think his character represents? Is he ultimately a helpful figure, or does he signify a false solution to life's problems?

4. When describing themselves, the protagonists speak mostly of their inadequacies and low self-esteem. Yet they eventually reveal a deep love for one another. What do the outside perspectives of Stanzi, China, and Lansdale reveal about their true abilities?

5. Do you believe that the characters send bomb threats to the school? If so, why do you think they do it?

6. When Stanzi and Gustav travel to the Place of Arrivals, they expect to find a land of geniuses—a paradise free of tests and absentee parents. Instead, they come to realize that the community is equally oppressive and its inhabitants look down on the outside world. What do you think this land represents?

7. Patricia is the only adult narrator and she appears later than the other main characters. Her full backstory is never revealed, but she is instrumental in helping Stanzi and Gustav realize the dangers of the Place of Arrivals. Why do you think A.S. King includes her perspective?

8. Near the end of the novel, China states in upside-down text, "The world will be upside down forever. We have to come to terms with this." What does this statement suggest about her path toward healing?

9. How do you interpret the novel's title?

10. Rather than telling the story in a straightforward manner, King creates an incredibly surreal and dreamlike universe. Why might she have decided to frame the novel this way? What are the benefits of this writing style?

About the Author

A.S. King is the highly acclaimed author of *Glory O'Brien's History of the Future*, which was a *New York Times Book Review* Editors' Choice, received six starred reviews, and appeared on ten best-of-the-year lists; *Reality Boy*, which received five starred reviews, was featured on seven end-of-year "best" lists, and was a YALSA Best Fiction for Young Adults book; *Ask the Passengers*, which was a Los Angeles Times Book Prize winner, received six starred reviews, appeared on ten end-of-year "best" lists, and was a Lambda Literary Award finalist; and *Everybody Sees the Ants*, which received six starred reviews, was an Andre Norton Award finalist, and was a YALSA Top Ten Best Fiction for Young Adults book. She is also the author of the Edgar Award–nominated, Michael L. Printz Honor Book *Please Ignore Vera Dietz* and *The Dust of 100 Dogs*, an ALA Best Book for Young Adults. When asked about her writing, King says, "Some people don't know if my characters are crazy or if they are experiencing something magical. I think that's an accurate description of how I feel every day." She lives in Pennsylvania with her husband and children, and she invites you to visit her website at as-king.com.